A School Inspector Calls

by

Rosie Cavendish

Miss Clover Lightfoot Murder Mystery No.1

Dedication

To all teachers, everywhere.

.

A tiny primer for the curious

ONCE UPON A TIME…

Schools in the UK were inspected by individual local inspectors.
These inspectors held the title of Her Majesty's Inspectors of Schools, or HMIs.
In 1992 the government created an additional organisation to conduct audits of entire schools.
The new inspection organisation was called *The Office for Standards in Education* or
Ofsted.

"Light the warning beacons, Ofsted are coming!"

Headline in a teaching magazine, 1996

1

Miss Clover Lightfoot nodded and smiled, concealing her exasperation effortlessly. She sat at one of the child-sized tables in her classroom that was, by coincidence, the table that the children referred to as *the clever table*. Not that she thought of it that way herself. It was simply a table where she sometimes seated children who found it easy to get on with their work without demanding much of her attention. However, opposite Clover sat three distinguished people all of whom, she noted, thought themselves very clever indeed and none of whom showed signs of getting on with their work without a great deal of her attention.

The first of her visitors was Mrs Amanda Chapman, Head Inspector of Schools for the shiny, new organisation known as *The Office for Standards in Education*, or *Ofsted*, for short. Mrs Chapman, a small woman with a neat, round face and neat, round spectacles to match, had been talking passionately, without interruption, for more than ten minutes and showed no sign of concluding whatever point she was trying to make. If anything, her rhetoric had become even more hyperbolic as the minutes continued to tick by. The zeal with which she spoke and the slightly wild gleam in her eye might have troubled Miss Lightfoot even more if it weren't for the other two people present.

Beside Mrs Chapman sat the august figure of Dr Arthur Winter, Chief of *Her Majesty's Inspectorate of Schools*, a completely different organisation from Mrs Chapman's newfangled *Ofsted* outfit. *Her Majesty's Inspectorate* was a much older institution and Dr Winter himself was a figure of almost legendary renown with a very different perspective from Mrs Chapman on most things. This much was made obvious by his none-too-discreet eye-rolling and his occasional emission of an exhausted sigh.

Finally, sitting in the ample shadow of Dr Winter, both literally and figuratively, was Antonia Reynolds, the waspish Deputy Chief of *Her Majesty's Inspectorate* and second-in-command to Dr Winter. Antonia, who liked to be addressed informally by her first name, was widely considered to be the power behind Dr Winter's considerable throne. Unseen by the two more senior inspectors, she met Miss Lightfoot's eye and gave her a sympathetic grin, as if to say, 'I, at least, understand what you're going through.'

The purpose of this meeting was notionally for Clover to receive feedback about her teaching from the visiting school inspectors but Mrs Chapman was far from concise when expressing her views and the discussion had ranged far and wide, sometimes getting quite heated along the way. The longer the meeting went on, the clearer it became to Clover that, despite her best efforts, the feedback she was receiving was not at all good. Mrs Chapman took a sip from her glass of water and appeared poised to continue but Dr Winter took advantage of her brief silence and made a noise with his lips that sounded like a resentful motorboat. This, it seemed, was his way of indicating he had something to add to the discussion.

Mrs Chapman did not concede the floor gracefully but she turned her head and addressed Dr Winter as she finished her point, 'Schools should be palaces of learning!' she said passionately, 'I think we are all very much agreed on that point are we not? Surely our classrooms should not be places where children are forced to squat under a blanket when it is time for them to read a book.' She jabbed a finger at the arrangement of bookshelves and blankets in the corner of Clover's classroom. She paused then, glaring at Dr Winter who blinked before replying.

'Oh, indubitably. An important point well made, Mrs Chapman,' he said, though he had an air of wanting to dismiss her comments quickly. 'However, before we condemn Miss Lightfoot's efforts completely, may we hear from you, Clover? Why have you have arranged your book corner in this manner?'

Dr Winter himself now gestured towards the corner of the room, where Clover had constructed her somewhat unusual book corner. Undeniably, it had the appearance of a slightly odd-looking bivouac, made from a soft, purple blanket, that had been suspended on lengths of string between two small bookshelves. This had created a concealed den in which children could hide out and read while enjoying a little privacy. All of the children in Clover's class had, at one time or another, enjoyed crawling inside the little nook with a book, knowing that they would be completely hidden from view. If anyone approached to peer inside, they would find a tiny, cushion-filled hidey-hole, flooded with light from the floor-to-ceiling windows which provided ample light for reading and afforded the tiny space a pleasing view out towards the playground and the playing field beyond.

'Of course, I'd be delighted to explain my thinking,' said Clover, surprised to hear the sound of her own voice after keeping silent for so long. 'I know that it may be a little unusual for children of this age to be offered a secluded space to read but I believe it really helps for the children to be able to read privately sometimes.'

Mrs Chapman turned her glare towards Clover, 'And what evidence do you have that such an odd and potentially dangerous cranny provides any benefit to the children's learning at all?'

'Well, personally, I find that the chance to read alone, in a peaceful, private space can really change the way that I experience a book,' said Clover sincerely. 'Having some privacy helps me absorb the words and reflect on the meaning. Being given the time and space to truly understand a book in this way, can turn reading into that wonderful trans-formative experience that we all hope for when we pick up a good book. Having a lovely time reading like that can change a child's outlook on their learning completely. It might even change the course of their whole life.'

'Fiddlesticks!' said Mrs Chapman, unable to contain herself any longer. 'Pure tosh! This is exactly the kind of speculative nonsense that leads to classes spending an entire year studying only facts and figures that relate to *dragons*.'

This last comment was a reference to another teacher in the school, Miss Lightfoot's good friend and colleague Ellie Robinson who taught an excessively large class of 6 year-olds in Year 1. Clover always took criticism of her own teaching very seriously. Indeed, she always sought to learn from any advice she was offered, but she didn't feel comfortable letting harsh words about her best friend pass unchallenged and she opened her mouth to say something in Ellie's defence.

However, before Clover could utter a sound, Dr Winter cleared his throat and took charge of the meeting. When he spoke his voice had a new edge to it and he addressed Mrs Chapman with all the gruff authority of an irritable bear. 'Amanda,' he said sternly, 'if you are referring to the work of Miss Robinson in Year 1, then I would caution you to speak to that particular young lady about the very intricate way in which she plans her teaching. To the *less experienced* observer, it may well seem that there is an excessive enjoyment of fictional lizards in her chosen manner of addressing the curriculum, but if you take the time to understand her work then I think you will be most impressed.'

The words *less experienced* carried such an implied insult of Mrs Chapman's judgement that it stopped her in her tracks. She bristled and shot a glare at Dr Winter that contrived to say, 'How *dare* you?'

For a few seconds Mrs Chapman's furious silence seemed to be deeply satisfying to Dr Winter and he smiled, allowing the uncomfortable moment to continue a little longer. Eventually, he closed his eyes and took a deep breath as he finally conceded the need to make peace. 'My dear Mrs Chapman, shall we discuss this in private before we take matters any further?' he asked. Looking daggers at him, Mrs Chapman agreed with a surly nod. Dr Winter turned to Clover and said, 'Miss Lightfoot, you're a fine young professional and I look forward to giving you some further feedback about your lesson at a later date, thank you for inviting us into your classroom today.'

'Quite,' said Mrs Chapman, shortly, and all four adults seated at *the clever table* rose from their seats to go their separate ways. Mrs Chapman and Dr Winter left together, talking in urgent, angry whispers and Antonia Reynolds excused herself silently with an encouraging nod to Miss Lightfoot.

Clover gratefully gathered up the three empty coffee mugs left behind by her visitors and headed for the staffroom. She was terribly behind with her preparations for the opening performance of the school play that would take place later on that very evening. The play was to go ahead despite the disruption of not one but two rival inspectorates deciding to inspect her school at the same time. It might have been reasonable to expect one of the organisations to reschedule but it seemed that they both considered themselves too important to be swayed by such considerations. Both teams of inspectors had been visiting the school and observing everything that took place for almost two weeks. Now, the different inspectors appeared to be at each other's throats and the school was caught in the middle. It was terrible timing, thought Clover, as she contemplated all the things that she needed to do for the evening's performance to go well. Bravely, she considered that it would all be over soon. Later that evening there would be a meeting with the parents where the inspectors would report their findings and after that they would finally leave. It could all be so much worse.

Little did she suspect that within a few short hours, one of the school inspectors would be dead and the foul crime of murder would be all that occupied her thoughts. It certainly never crossed her mind that it would fall to her, Miss Clover Lightfoot, to catch a murderer and save the day.

2

All the inspectors that now roamed the school had promised to stay out of the staffroom so that the teachers could have their break times in peace. But it had come to Miss Lightfoot's attention that peaceful breaks were not what the staffroom was being used for at all these days.

During the terrifying times when inspectors were prowling the corridors with clipboards and dangerously difficult questions, the staffroom had become a zone of furtive activity occupied by any teacher with something to hide. Clover had seen some teachers actually running, or trotting as quickly as dignity allowed, for the safety of the staffroom once the school bell rang. Once they were inside its walls, teachers wore a look of relief that might have been seen on the faces of fearful peasants sheltering from monsters in the holy precincts of a church. Like the vampires of legend, the inspectors could not enter unless some fool invited them in.

This meant that all manner of teachers who would previously have indulged their hermit-like tendencies and kept to their classrooms could now be found in the staffroom at strange times of the working day, all of them doing things that they didn't particularly want the inspectors to see.

Clover had seen more than one teacher in the act of retrospectively scattering ticks through the long-neglected practice-books that the children had been doodling in throughout the year. That was an uncomfortable escalation in attention-to-detail and it had crossed her mind that perhaps she should do the same with the practice books in her own classroom. She dismissed this with a shudder, it was pure paranoia.

Nobody had told the teachers that every book the children ever touched should be carefully marked, indeed, in Clover's opinion that wasn't actually appropriate. Who, as an adult or a child, would expect every aspect of their lives to be under the scrutiny of an omniscient, Orwellian mentor, ready to pounce on one's every errant thought? No, adults and children alike should be given time and space, indeed even whole books, in which they could work things out on their own.

The chances were that no inspector would even glance at any class's practice books for more than a second or two. However, Miss Lightfoot had to concede that such books did look so much better for a judiciously placed, entirely random, tick or two, here or there, just a speedy, hearty, devil-may-care mark made by a flying, fat, red pen. A mark deposited somewhere on the page, not referring to anything specific, could make whatever the child had done look like an acceptable mess rather than a shameful one.

As a teacher, nobody would actually tell you how much and how often you should mark your children's books. However, every teacher Miss Lightfoot knew lived with the constant lurking presence of their finest possible selves, a shadowy figure, haunting them accusingly with the silent implication that they could have done more or worked harder for every single child, every single day.

At this late hour, the staff room was only occupied by three people. Tom Flint, who was teaching the Year 4s this year, was sitting quietly in the corner typing something onto the new computer that had been set up there to make the staffroom seem up-to-date. He was completely absorbed in his activities, alternating between thoughtfully squinting at the screen and tending to the afflictions of the enormous printer beside him that made chirruping and grinding sounds whenever it wasn't jammed.

The other two people in the room were Mrs Janet Clegg, the school's deputy headteacher and Mr Simon Fish, the headteacher.

Clover found Janet likeable in a distant way and they exchanged nods as Clover made her way to the ever-bubbling urn to make herself a quick cup of tea. Janet was referred to as *Cleggy* by some of the older boys, who were practising being disrespectful ahead of going off to secondary school. If the school had anything like an enforcer it was certainly Janet. Errant children were constantly being threatened with being sent to Mrs Clegg.

Janet was usually dressed in either a power suit with a red jacket that she'd been wearing since the 80s, or in a vivid tracksuit that defied the eye with several garish shades of neon. She was a northerner and had an accent that a practised ear could identify as coming from Burnley. When Janet wanted to, she played up to this and her accent definitely became broader. This happened most noticeably when managing the school football team. Evoking the great footballing culture of northern England she bullishly bellowed things like 'Man on!' and 'Our ball ref!' in such an authoritative way that she usually got what she wanted, despite being relegated to the sidelines.

Clover respected Janet and thanked the heavens daily that there was someone at the school prepared to take on all of that stuff. For her part, Janet understood how difficult it was to be a class teacher and loyally waded into all manner of trouble to help her colleagues whenever help was needed.

Simon, the headteacher, was an entirely different kettle of fish. Mr Fish was not a fortunate name for a teacher, thought Clover. There was something inherently comedic about it, like a name from a picture book for very young children or a character in a Monty Python sketch. That said, using any name regularly enough, particularly in a school where routine was everywhere, could easily change the character of a sound. Had Mr Fish been a respected leader, his name would quickly have taken on the mystique of dignity that can surround even the strangest combination of phonemes, given time and consistent supporting evidence.

This was not, however, what had happened to Mr Fish. Simon was prone to equivocation. Clover found him to be an entirely reasonable, lovely man and yet what he was persuaded of one minute could, in another minute, be entirely reversed. This was not a good trait for the leader of a school and very often people would end up going to Janet to find out '*what Simon had decided*'. By this they meant to discover what Janet had decided that Simon should have decided. This arrangement saved face for everyone and sufficed perfectly well in peacetime but now that the inspectors had been amongst them for two weeks the relationship was showing signs of strain.

Strain may have been putting it too mildly. As Clover looked across the staffroom towards him, Simon seemed positively irate. Though he was trying to keep his voice down, it sounded more like a stage whisper when he spoke and he was almost shouting. 'Why are there two inspectorates here at once anyway?' 'Why should we have to put up with the HMIs and Ofsted at the same time? It's ridiculous!'

This gave Clover pause for thought. Dr Winter's HMIs - this acronym shortened *Her Majesty's Inspectors* to something that could be manageably referenced - were certainly duplicating the work of Mrs Chapman's *Ofsted* inspectors.

'Well of course the answer is obvious,' said Simon answering his own question. 'We're to be made an example of by both of them. We're entirely doomed.'

'Simon,' said Janet brusquely, 'would you prefer me to slap you or throw a glass of water in your face? You're starting to sound hysterical.' Janet looked across at Clover and Tom to see whether they were listening. They were of course, but both of them were doing a good impression of minding their own business. Janet continued, 'This whole inspection isn't even about us, it's all about politics. Don't you see? Dr Winter and his HMIs have a reputation for being cosy with the schools they inspect because they've been doing it a long time, so the government created *Ofsted* to challenge them and shake things up a bit. The two inspectorates were bound to clash eventually, it just so happens that the clash is here and now.'

'Do you think they're going to compete to see who can be the toughest on us?' said Simon. His expression took on a hunted look. 'I get a bad feeling about all of this. They're like circling wolves. The only question is who's going to take the biggest bite.'

'You can scare yourself all you like,' said Janet, 'but I think this is really about who inspects the inspectors and who's top dog between the two of them. All we can do is our best. The rest is their business. Anyway, I don't think it will be so bad. Dr Winter and the HMIs have been inspecting schools for years, they're not going to be unreasonable with us so Mrs Chapman and *Ofsted* will look silly if they disagree completely.' Simon didn't look convinced but Janet leaned closer and added, confidentially, 'Did you know that Mrs Chapman used to be an HMI herself? She was one of Dr Winter's most trusted deputies before she was appointed to run *Ofsted*. She's no fool, even if she is somewhat...motivated.'

'By *motivated* you mean barking mad,' said Simon, shaking his head. 'She talked to me for two hours this morning; I was trying to explain to her that some of the Year 3 children are actually quite charming, even if they are a bit wayward sometimes. I mean, they set fire to that hamster by accident; they were trying to keep it warm. I tried to explain that their hearts were in the right place and they were just trying to bring some genuine warmth into the world, but she just said she didn't have time for "*specious epithets*". In the same sentence she kept on talking about wanting children to have *targets*. I'd be a lot happier if her favourite metaphor wasn't about things that are only there to be shot at.'

'It's just the way everyone is talking nowadays,' said Janet, momentarily allowing Simon's gloom to affect her.

'My class are working on Shakespeare and portmanteau words,' interrupted Clover. 'You know, where you compress words together to make something new. Shakespeare was doing it long before Lewis Carroll. Anyway, I can't help thinking that *Ofsted* sounds like an abbreviation of *Off with their heads.*' She smiled ruefully and Tom laughed at the expression that appeared on Mr Fish's face. 'Sorry Simon, I'm only teasing,' said Clover, 'I'm sure their bark is much worse than their bite.'

Clover's smile was infectious and as he looked at her Simon's panic evaporated. He matched her smile and, out of his eye line, Janet gave Clover a sincere nod of thanks. Clover continued, 'I'm not really worried either. I agree with Janet, the inspectors seem more interested in each other than us.' She looked at Simon thoughtfully, 'I suppose what you say to the parents tonight will really help everyone understand the situation. It's going to be quite an unusual evening to have a big meeting right after the school play, but I can see why it makes sense to do it when all the parents are together. What they hear from you tonight will probably set the tone for how everyone thinks about all of this.'

A parade of expressions made their way across Mr Fish's face, beginning with the panic of realising that he hadn't been thinking about the late night meeting between the parents and the inspectors. This was quickly followed by the embarrassment of forgetting about the play that Miss Lightfoot's class were performing beforehand. Both of these realisations were followed by a look of concentration as he reassembled his composure.

'Janet,' he said firmly, 'I was actually just about to ask for your help with that speech, would you come and work with me in my office?' He turned to Clover. 'Miss Lightfoot, I do wish you the very best of luck with the play, I'm so sorry I haven't been able to attend a rehearsal, it will all...go well...I trust?'

'It will be a proper reflection of the children's achievements,' said Clover, 'I know you've always said you believe that a performance which enhances the children's learning is far more valuable than creating some kind of showy, overly-polished spectacle.'

'Oh yes. Exactly. Yes,' said Mr Fish, still hesitating by the door, unsure if he'd ever said anything of the kind.

'Shall we decide on what to say to the parents?' prompted Janet. Simon snapped out of his new-found worry about what might be in Clover's play and focused back on what he needed to do next. 'Indeed, after you,' he said, waving her onwards.

Tom sat back from the computer and laughed, 'Do you enjoy pulling their strings or do you only do it when you really think they deserve it?' he asked.

Clover stirred her tea and smiled, 'Oh they just need a little nudge from time to time,' she said. 'They mean well. It's just that trying to do too many things at once makes anyone seem stupid.'

'You've got that right,' said Tom. 'I was trying to create some notices while I was finishing off some marking but I ended up not doing either.' He shook his head, 'I shouldn't have bothered trying to use this beastly printer, I could have handwritten the notices I'm trying to print in a tenth of the time.'

'Isn't it working?' asked Clover sympathetically.

'I think it's working fine,' said Tom, 'but I'm definitely not using it correctly. It's only printing half a word on each page.' He held up the sheets of paper for her amusement. 'I could have stopped messing with it ages ago but I got curious and ended up going down a rabbit hole about *print protocols*, whatever they are.'

'And what are they?' asked Clover perching on one of the staffroom chairs.

'Well, I've discovered that they are actually a gigantic waste of time,' said Tom, turning off the computer. 'Is your play going to be…?'

'…a disaster,' Clover said, 'oh yes, unashamedly so. It will be very jolly and the children have really learned from the experience and that's all that matters.'

'Quite right. I hear that Andrew is one of the witches?'

'Yes and he's fabulous in the role, you wait and see.'

'He didn't want to be a warlock?'

'No, he wants to be a witch. We had a chat about it and he's adamant. His Mum and Dad are quite happy about it too.'

'It sounds like he's having a great time. You do have a talent for unleashing the children on the world, you know.'

Clover sighed, 'I only fear that the world has come to meet them this time around. They were supposed to be doing their own versions of scenes from Shakespeare but the mood has been so grim during the inspections that the ones they've chosen are focused on betrayal, death, destruction and curses.'

'It all sounds very properly Shakespearian to me,' said Tom.

'He did write one or two plays about love too, you know,' said Clover, daring a small smile in Tom's direction.

Tom considered her words carefully but his eyes were focusing on his internal analysis of the question. 'I tend to think of the sonnets rather than the plays when I think about Shakespeare writing in that way,' he said innocently.

Clover sipped her tea, not bothering to mask her exasperation this time, it didn't seem like Tom was going to notice. She changed the subject, 'What do you think's going to happen with the inspections?' she asked.

'Well, your play will be the last act before they're over,' said Tom, renewing his grin. 'From what I understand, the Parent Teacher Association are putting on some drinks to warm everyone up and then Mrs Chapman will give *Ofsted's* feedback to us in person before she submits her report before midnight tonight.'

'Such theatrics!' said Clover. 'What's Dr Winter going to do about that?'

'Oh he'll stay for the play and then he'll be off home to bed. He said he'd fax his report over to the school office before he's done for the night but he's not about to face up to those the parents personally; they can be quite intimidating as a group.'

'*The sight of blood to crowds begets the thirst of more, As the first wine-cup leads to the long revel*,' quoted Miss Lightfoot.

'Is that Shakespeare?' asked Tom.

'Byron actually, but he's more famous for writing about love than violence.' She raised an eyebrow at him.

'Huh,' said Tom thoughtfully, 'Do you really think it's going to get that ugly, tonight? With all the parents there, I mean?'

Clover sighed, 'Yes Tom, I think it might become very ugly indeed.'

3

Returning to her classroom, Clover found that some of the children had arrived early to prepare for the evening performance. The twins, Josh and Jake, were there but to her surprise she found that they were actually making their preparations quite peacefully. This was because their mother, Bettina, had very ably separated them by packing the boys' costumes in two separate bags which she'd deposited in different areas of the classroom.

It wasn't that the twins disliked each other, neither was it the case that they were particularly difficult boys, they simply got in each other's way sometimes and when that happened it provoked extraordinary battles. It seemed like every tiny interaction they participated in needed to be totalled up in terms of an eternal reckoning of profit and loss between the two of them, this being the only way to ensure that everything was fair.

Clover had grasped the dynamic between the boys very quickly and she had adapted her practices accordingly, arranging group activities to prevent the boys competing against each other directly and helping them each develop wider circles of friends. In achieving this, Clover had won an adoring friend and powerful ally in Bettina Williams. As well as being the twins' mother, Bettina was also the Chairperson of the Parent Teacher Association and an influential character in many circles. Other parents and teachers had tried various ways to win her friendship but only Clover had truly succeeded. This wasn't something that Clover had ever anticipated, in fact she only realised it had occurred when they were already getting along famously. By then, Clover had quietly come to understand why Bettina had involved herself so completely in the PTA in the first place. Her life had been taken over by supporting her boys and she had simply gone along with it, immersing herself in the lives of her children and their school.

Clover often found herself constantly feeling a sense of compassion whenever she encountered Bettina. Bettina coped with so much, so well, and Clover was used to coping with a great many things too. The two of them shared the practical understanding of what it was like to prioritise the needs of others ahead of themselves and this fact alone was enough for them to feel quite unguarded and sisterly towards each other. As Clover entered the classroom, Bettina was fully occupied trying to help Josh arrange his toga and Clover smiled to herself at the prospect of seeing a friendly face.

Bettina and the boys weren't alone in the classroom. At a central table, three girls from Clover's class were talking excitedly and simultaneously about their costumes. The three, Holly, Olivia and Chloe, made up a fearsome triumvirate that was certainly the governing force in the social lives of the other girls in the class. They had reacted with identical expressions of horror at Clover's suggestion that they might enjoy playing the part of the three witches from Macbeth.

Instead, the three girls had settled on playing the three daughters of King Lear. Olivia's mother, Sandy Delaney, who had a reputation for making her feelings known, had come to talk to Clover about this.

'Olivia assures me that they've read the play but I think they've only actually read Act One,' Sandy had said in a confiding whisper, though she and Clover had been absolutely alone at the time of her visit.

'Yes, I did suspect that was the case,' Clover had replied gently, 'I do think they're really going to learn a lot from this.'

'So...you intend to let them continue without realising that Goneril and Regan are both treacherous, power-crazed psychopaths who come to a nasty end and that the role my daughter has chosen culminates in her character's suicide?'

'They're very sensitive subjects to deal with, it's true,' Clover had replied thoughtfully. 'It's always a struggle not to neuter Shakespeare when teaching it to children and there are distinctly adult themes to be explored. But that said, I'd like to respect the girls' choices in picking out this play and let them learn about the way these glamorous characters harbour unpalatable contradictions. I'm sure they'll start to understand the implications of their choices very quickly as they research their roles in more depth.'

This had indeed proved to be the case and while Holly and Chloe had eventually taken up the roles of Goneril and Regan, Olivia had, at the last moment and possibly at the behest of her mother, decided that the fairy spirit Ariel, from The Tempest, would make a much more appropriate role for her.

However, it seemed that Olivia's source material for the choice of Ariel owed more to the character of the same name from the animated movie, *The Little Mermaid*, than to anything from Shakespeare. This had given rise to yet another layer of interesting lessons to learn about composition, decision-making and compromise, all of which Clover was happy to facilitate.

The resultant scene that had emerged from the girls' work was an extraordinary hybrid piece in which three sisters - one of whom is additionally managing mermaid issues - decide that friendship, and possibly magic, are far more important than the rules that their father might have arbitrarily made up for them to follow. The arc of the new scene dwelt heavily on a sorrowful beginning in which the girls were oppressed by the practical limitations that boring old King Lear had placed on them. These various injustices included severely limiting the swimming activities of the mermaid and curtailing the pocket money of the other princesses to a reprehensible degree. The scene culminated in the girls joining forces to discover a technicality in the rules which they ruthlessly exploited, persuading King Lear to change his mind. It ended with all three of them granted wealth and dominion over all the lands of the kingdom, and indeed, in the case of the mermaid, over the previously neutral international waters that surrounded it.

'All adaptations bring something new to a play,' Clover had explained to Sandy Delaney when she had come to visit her a second time. 'The girls will definitely learn about King Lear as well but for now, they've written a story which has a beginning, a middle and an end. They have practised and refined their scene to a point where they're ready to perform it. I think that we should enjoy what they've composed on its own terms.'

'And what does Mr Fish think about that?' Sandy had asked pointedly, with such unexpected venom that Clover had been forced to smother a giggle. Something about the juxtaposition of Olivia the errant mermaid and the sudden evocation of the overarching authority of 'Mr Fish' had almost been her undoing.

Clover managed to keep a cool head and sweetly suggested to Sandy that she make an appointment to chat to Mr Fish about it in his capacity as headteacher. Mr Fish, Clover assured her, would be only too happy to discuss the matter at length and Clover herself would help the girls abide by whatever he decided.

Mr Fish and Mrs Clegg had joined forces to meet with Sandy and, largely because of Janet Clegg's steely sense of what was best for the children's learning, Sandy's plea for the performance to become something 'more traditional' had been overruled. Unbeknownst to Clover this decision was quite a coup and word rang forth through the parent body that Miss Lightfoot had actually managed to put Sandy Delaney in her place.

This kind of rumour couldn't have been further from Clover's intent and now she found herself breathing a quiet sigh of relief that she didn't have to face Sandy Delaney at that particular moment. Clover went to see if the girls needed any help but she involuntarily jumped as she saw who was on the floor behind their table.

Sandy Delaney was down on her hands and knees trying to fix the hem of Olivia's mermaid's tail and she looked up briefly before returning to her work without meeting Clover's eye. Clover spoke first to break the tension, 'Oh, hello Sandy, is everything alright?' asked Clover, 'let me see if I can help.' Not waiting for a reply. Clover ducked down beside Sandy to help with fixing the hem. She focused on the task at hand. The tail's stuffing wasn't going to stay tucked in no matter how it was arranged. Clover suggested some safety pins from her desk that might do the trick. She went to fetch them and when she returned, with a very soft tone in her voice, she praised Olivia's rather sumptuous costume purposefully mentioning that it was fit for any role Olivia might ever wish to play. Sandy gave her a conciliatory nod but with her lip very much bitten, as if she might have said a great deal more on the subject.

One of the reasons that Sandy usually got what she wanted was that Sandy was the Chair of the school's Board of

Governors, a very serious position indeed. The board of governors had the final say on anything the school did that wasn't regulated by the government and, ultimately, the board would be responsible for replacing the headteacher, should anything terrible happen to him, though it would never usually come to such a thing, not in normal circumstances at any rate.

Clover looked up from helping with Olivia's dress to see another member of her class standing doubtfully at the classroom door. 'Sequoia,' called Clover, beckoning to the girl to come inside. 'Have you got everything you need?' Sequoia was a bright-eyed but very quiet girl who was so sensitive to the thoughts and wishes of her peers that she sometimes censored herself out of anything but agreement with them. Sequoia and Clover had forged a bond almost instantly when Clover had found her spontaneously tidying up after some of the other girls and gently intervened to suggest she might like to have a read in the secluded reading nook instead. Sequoia hadn't replied but had nodded with the urgency of someone seizing upon a very secret wish coming true. Since then, she had been quietly but fiercely loyal to her teacher and looked to Miss Lightfoot with an unconditional respect that Clover struggled to feel worthy of.

'Have you got a copy of your lines?' asked Clover. Sequoia was holding a plastic bag with her costume in it but she didn't seem to have a copy of the script. 'Shall I find you another copy or will you be able to share?' Clover asked. Sequoia shrugged off the question with a smile but she didn't say anything. Instead she glanced at the reading den in the book corner. 'Why don't you get changed in there?' Clover suggested. Sequoia didn't need to be asked twice and she vanished from view.

'Do you ever get the urge to hide in there and have a cry?' asked a voice behind her. Clover turned to find her friend Bettina grinning at her mischievously. 'It's just that I could use a turn at that myself,' she said with a giggle.

'Actually, who goes inside is something that the children work out between themselves,' Clover smiled. 'Being fair to everyone doesn't have to mean the same as treating everyone exactly equally...except when it comes to Josh and Jake, of course.'

'Well those inspectors had better be fair to you all here at the school or there'll be trouble,' said Bettina conspiratorially. 'I was approached by quite a few of the other parents with the idea of picketing the school gates to keep the inspectors out.'

Clover smiled, 'Oh no, inspections aren't that bad. We are all professionals and we should welcome people giving us feedback about what we do.'

'Of course,' said Bettina seriously. 'But there's feedback and there are hatchet jobs.'

'Hatchet jobs?' asked Clover incredulously. 'Even if people have their issues to deal with, I really don't think that anyone who's working in education would ever want to do a school any harm.'

'I'm not so sure,' said Sandy, looking up from Olivia's dress. She nodded a hello to Bettina, 'I've been hearing the same rumours as you,' she said. 'From the questions that certain inspectors have been asking the parents, it sounds as if they've already decided that the school is no good and they're going to make sure everyone knows it.' Clover took a second to be thankful that Mr Fish hadn't been exposed to such rumours. Hearing that his worst nightmares were about to come true would be enough to turn what remained of his confidence to dust.

'Which inspectors?' asked Clover, curiously.

'Well that's just it, not the ones that you might think,' Sandy replied. 'As Chair of Governors, I've seen the previous reports that Dr Winter has written about the school and they're all quite glowing, but he asked Fiona Beacon what she'd do if the children failed these new standardised tests they have.'

'But we don't do the standardised tests,' said Clover, 'we've always refused to do them. They're not statutory and, even if they were, they're practically meaningless. How can you possibly define a child's ability with a single number? It's like trying to describe the features of a mountain by measuring the height of its peak. A measurement like that doesn't tell you much about the mountain that's of any use to anyone.'

'Miss Lightfoot,' said Bettina teasingly, 'what a beautiful image, I didn't know you had such a poetic soul. If you don't think test scores mean anything then you should see the showdown you caused in my house when Jake scored higher than Josh in last week's spelling test.'

Clover tried to lighten her tone but she was quite firm about her reasons for anything she did and she wanted to be sure Bettina and Sandy both knew it. 'That particular test had a purpose,' she said. 'I wanted everyone to focus on particular words invented by Shakespeare and how much they've embedded themselves in everyday language. I wouldn't presume to tell the children that the mark they received from that test told them anything more than how they'd done on that test on that day.'

'That's all very well while they're here with you,' said Sandy, mildly, 'but when they move on to other places, people are going to want to know what they're capable of.' This was a thorny issue. Everyone knew that Sandy intended to send Olivia to a private school in a year's time, Sandy had been very outspoken about it. Olivia was already being tutored during the evenings and at weekends to ensure she could pass the entrance exams. Clover kept her opinions to herself about this but privately she thought that teaching someone to pass a test was wasting a child's opportunities to learn far more important things. She took a breath.

'Everyone's tired and tensions are running high right now but believe me, tests really aren't that important and nobody's going to be the victim of a hatchet job. Everyone will behave very professionally, I'm sure,' she said although she was by no means as sure as she made herself sound.

4

As the rest of the children arrived Miss Lightfoot took the chance to speak to the children away from their parents before they made their way to the hall. She told herself that this was so that she could try to calm them down a little. However, once she looked at them as a group, she could see that they were much calmer than she was. 'Whose parents are coming tonight?' she asked and every hand in the class was immediately raised. She swallowed, her throat had become quite dry.

The children sat in the same chairs that they used during a normal working day but, to Clover, everything had taken on a slightly dreamlike quality. Whether they or their parents had intended it, the children's costumes had all taken on a little of the individual child's own character. To the insightful Miss Lightfoot, this made some of the children look like tiny caricatures of themselves, or possibly, in some cases, caricatures of their parents. Little witches abounded, Clover counted five of them, a group of very sensible girls who always sat together were now revealed to be a clandestine coven. Their sweet, earnest faces were all painted the same shade of pea-green under their matching, plastic, conical hats and they exchanged glances gleefully when Clover wasn't looking.

There were a great many princely, mock-tudor boys dressed in a more obviously improvised manner. Their costumes consisted of radically cropped pillowcases and duvet covers, selected for their opulent patterns and regal colours. These innocent fabrics had been further given the look of tunics by means of gathering them at the waist with a thin ladies belt or a piece of string. Odd pieces of their mother's costume jewellery were also worn by many of them to evoke a sense of foppish grandeur.

On the tables in front of the children, instead of their usual workbooks, were small mounds of plastic bags for their costumes, adorned with crumpled copies of the script. The classroom's high windows, which usually let light pour into the room, had turned black with the coming of night. The faint reflections in the glass caught the attention of some of the children, their gaze straying to meet the eyes of their ghostly counterpart staring back at them. Miss Lightfoot, by contrast, was dressed in her usual smartly-casual way, which in some way only added to the oddity of the situation.

'Isn't it strange to be here together in the evening,' Clover commented, addressing the whole class. 'Everything's so different, but familiar too, it reminds me of Alice Through the Looking Glass, though I'm sure it's not going to be anything like as scary as that.' Sequoia nodded seriously at this, giving Clover her complete attention. She looked like a warrior taking final instructions before going into battle.

'Just remember,' said Clover softly, 'whatever funny meetings the adults are having tonight, the most important thing that's happening is that you're putting on your play. You've practised your scenes so many times that you could practically do them in your sleep. Don't worry about anything, just focus on whatever you have to do next and enjoy it. I'm so proud of all the work you've done, I know everyone in the audience is going to absolutely love seeing what you've come up with.' Clover gave them a conspiratorial smile and then asked them to line up by the classroom door, putting her trust in them completely for what was to follow.

Chairs were laid out across two thirds of the school hall and they were gradually filling with parents. The final third of the space was to be used as the stage and it was lit brightly by four supremely dusty spotlights that were bolted to the hall's roof. The children filed in behind Clover, all of them eyeing the audience as they went, looking for their own parents among the growing number of people that were jealously guarding their preferred seats.

Entering the hall, Clover caught a glimpse of her friend, Ellie Robinson, peeking over the lid of the upright piano. Ellie was at her ease, playfully entertaining the gathering audience with some improvisations on well known pieces of music. Ellie had come back for the evening just to play accompaniments for the show, despite Year 1 having nothing directly to do with the night's proceedings. Buoyed up by the sound of the music, Clover gave Ellie a thankful nod as their eyes met. Ellie was an accomplished pianist and had developed the much needed skill of keeping up with children as they struggled to learn new songs. She could effortlessly vary the tempo and she knew how to emphasise the notes that would cue the singing at the start of a verse. At the moment, though, she was simply enjoying herself by extemporising a wandering meditation on fanfares and various unrelated tunes that took her from commonly sung school songs to archaic classical references. These were being played as much for her own amusement as the audience's.

As the children made their entrance, Ellie struck up a rousing tune, making Clover smile. This encouraged Ellie to change the tone of the music to a glowering minor key and

Clover had to stifle a giggle. Ellie pantomimed looking daggers in the direction of Mrs Chapman, who seemed oblivious to all the human activity in the hall as she divided her attention between an *Ofsted* form on her clipboard and taking notes about the various displays on the hall's walls.

Changing the tone again, Ellie swayed from side to side as she slid into Saint-Saëns' affectionate portrait of an elephant from *The Carnival of the Animals*. Clover followed Ellie's gaze this time to Dr Winter who, resoundingly elephantine in his manner, was positively wallowing in the attention of the parents. He was a well known and popular figure to them, familiar from his numerous media appearances and regarded as something as a local celebrity. This time Clover couldn't suppress a snigger. She also allowed herself to be properly amused by the sympathetic bobbing and bouncing that the children added to their walk as they paraded across the stage.

Clover was tempted to ask Ellie to slide across the piano stool so that they could play a duet, just for the fun of it. That year they had developed a party piece, Dvořák's *Slavonic Dance No. 8*. This was a piece so feisty and strutting that it always put Clover in an excellent mood. Unfortunately, this wasn't the time to indulge herself, such show boating would only distract from the children's performances and in Clover's mind the children were the only good reason for doing any of this.

Tom Flint waited quietly by the gym equipment at the back of the hall, looking vaguely troubled. He gave Clover a rather bleak smile that seemed to express sympathy. She could read his expression all too easily. Tom always wanted to be fixing something, regardless of whether that was the best way to improve matters or not. If only he wasn't so intent of formulating plans to set things straight, perhaps then he might start to see that the subtleties of a situation might be the most important things of all. Unfortunately, if any particular situation hadn't been clearly labelled then Tom seemed entirely unable even to notice it.

Clover saw her class safely to their places and they settled immediately, anticipating the delivery of their well-drilled performance. She allowed herself a moment to wander over to

Ellie and take a breath before proceedings got underway. There was very little she could do at this point to affect the way the play would turn out, indeed, she had organised things so that every element of the performance was led by the children. Being in the spotlight herself in any shape or form, was not for her and, in this context, every time she intervened in the performance she would be practically stealing an opportunity for a child to practice their speaking and listening in front of a large audience.

'Everything ready?' asked Ellie over the sound of her own playing.

'As far as the children are concerned, absolutely,' said Clover, 'heavens knows what the so-called adults will make of it. I'm beginning to wonder if the lot of them are more concerned with appearances than anything else.'

'Clover!' said Ellie, shocked, 'You're the one who's always telling me to ignore the nonsense and concentrate on the children. If I recall rightly, your words to me were something along the lines of, *all you have to do is really notice the good that you're doing for the children and they'll give you all the inspiration you need*. I think that's what you said but you were preoccupied polishing your halo at the time so I may have been mistaken.'

'*Urgh*,' said Clover, 'far too sweet, I sound sickening, how *do* you put up with me?'

'I binge on chocolate,' said Ellie snippily, 'discretely and in moderation, but with gusto, that's what you drive me to.' Ellie slid her sheet music to one side and revealed a slender bar of luxury dark chocolate waiting for her there. Clover snorted with involuntary laughter and the children all turned their heads towards her as one. She instantly sobered and smiled benevolently back at them. 'Is that *all* for you then?' she asked, nodding at the chocolate bar.

'Well, I might be persuaded to share a little of it,' Ellie beaming at her friend. 'We could hide behind the piano and scoff the lot.'

'Stop it or I might actually take you up on that.' Clover's heart had lightened and she looked around for somewhere to sit. She'd only be in the children's way if she tried to conceal herself somewhere on the stage but one of the parents had 'accidentally' settled himself in the seat she'd tried to reserve for herself. It was fine, she didn't feel like sitting anyway. That was when she noticed that she was being beckoned over by Dr Winter.

'Sit here my dear, won't you?' called Dr Winter in a fatherly manner, waving to the empty seat beside him. 'My delightful deputy, the relentlessly efficient Miss Reynolds, cannot be with me tonight so I am in need of a wise companion to inform me about what I am to witness this evening.'

'It is my hope that all will be entirely self-evident,' said Clover offering Dr Winter her best smile and starting to retreat.

'Please,' said Dr Winter, 'if you are not entirely occupied with your work and you would sit with me, you would be doing me a very good deed, Miss Lightfoot.' Clover looked around and quickly gathered what Dr Winter's motives might be.

With Antonia Reynolds absent, there was nobody to sit in the empty seat between him and the seat reserved for the fractious Mrs Chapman. It only occurred to Clover at that moment that Dr Winter might find Mrs Chapman so entirely objectionable that he would truly value Clover's intervention. She stopped hesitating and gave him a gentle smile. 'Of course, Dr Winter. I'd be delighted.'

'Thank you very much,' said Dr Winter, noting her understanding of the situation with satisfaction. 'I do wish this whole matter were much simpler.'

'I trust wisdom will prevail, Dr Winter,' said Clover generously.

'Indeed, the optimism of youth, Miss Lightfoot. When will the show begin?'

'Any moment,' said Clover, 'But I think Mr Fish has a few words to say first.'

Simon Fish made his way to the front of the hall and as Janet Clegg came up behind him the chatter in the audience faded away to nothing. 'Thank you, thank you everyone,' said Simon gratefully, obviously not cognisant of Janet's presence or her influence on the audience. 'It is with great pleasure that we welcome you all here tonight. Parents, children and our visiting Inspectors of Schools, who have been going to such lengths to

24

help us demonstrate our school's strengths during this soon-to-be-completed inspection process.'

Though obviously composed in haste, Simon's words still seemed overly-practised and awkward. This wasn't helped by Mrs Chapman wandering blithely across the front of the hall, passing directly in front of Mr Fish as he spoke. It wasn't that she pointedly ignored him or even that she was late to take her seat, other people were still settling down too, it was more that Mrs Chapman seemed to exude a sense of finding the whole school somehow distasteful. Simon put his dignity aside and was almost fawning over Mrs Chapman as he tried to gloss over the awkwardness of the moment. 'Thank you for coming,' he said again, with as much sincerity as he could manage. 'Thank you, both of you.' He looked between Dr Winter and Mrs Chapman, who were now seated on either side of Clover. 'Thank you for taking the time to think about what will really help our school the most, we'll be very keen to take up any of your recommendations on how we can do better, improving things for the children is all that matters to us in the end.' Janet nodded along with this: that was clearly the line that they'd agreed on together. Clover was impressed that Janet had managed to get Simon to focus on what was actually important rather than his fears, it was a good sign for everyone. 'With that,' said Simon, 'I'll hand over to Miss Lightfoot's class and we can see what they've been learning about this term.'

Clover, who was now stranded in the middle of the front row, started the polite round of applause. The rest of the audience dutifully followed as the children glanced at each other with eager smiles. Clover nodded to Sequoia, it was she who would speak first and set the rest of the performance going. As Sequoia rose to her feet and stepped into the middle of the stage area, Clover met her eyes. They were face to face and only separated by a few feet but Clover felt as if she were safely protected in the body of the audience whereas Sequoia stood alone and exposed in the glare of the lights. Clover nodded to her, silently offering her utmost encouragement.

Sequoia's head dropped and she looked at her shoes. Clover's breath caught in her throat. Sequoia had forgotten her lines. Clover blinked. Sequoia's hands were empty. She didn't have a copy of the script and Clover realised that she didn't have one either. Clover could remember most of the lines from the script off by heart because of their endless practices but Sequoia had preferred to practice her lines alone and Clover was drawing a blank. The other children couldn't help her either, the narrator's script was printed separately from the ones that they had in their hands, to save paper. If Sequoia couldn't remember what to say on her own then Clover would have to dash across to the piano and grab a copy of the script to see what she was supposed to say. Her heart was racing but she kept smiling, willing the girl on. It had been a gamble to give timid Sequoia this particular role but she would gain so much from facing an audience like this, if only she could keep her nerve. At least five seconds passed and became ten as the audience grew silent, concerned that something had gone wrong.

Sequoia lifted her head and her eyes flicked open in a single arresting movement. She stared into the faces of her audience with a self-possessiveness that Clover had never seen in the girl before.

'We know what we are,' said Sequoia, 'but not what we may be.' The girl's small voice sounded quiet in the hall but her words carried to the furthest corners.

For a moment, she seemed to be the very embodiment of youth, as if she were speaking about the potential of all the children on the stage and all that they might become. In her vulnerability she projected all the dignity that poor Mr Fish had failed to deliver. Sequoia felt the power of her own words and she managed a small smile as she looked around at the faces in the audience, all of them fixed on her. She seemed to grow an inch in height as she saw that she had captured their attention completely. Clover found herself wiping her eyes as she started to breathe again. Sequoia continued, gaining in confidence with every word, 'William Shakespeare wrote these lines for the character of Ophelia in his play *Hamlet*. One theme in *Hamlet* is how nobody can be sure about what will happen in their lives or what they might do in the future. We have been thinking about questions like this. We made up our own versions of Shakespeare's plays to help us think about why they are so interesting. We really hope you enjoy our show, thank you.' The applause from the audience was hearty this time.

'Impressive girl,' whispered Mrs Chapman unexpectedly.

'Yes,' Clover replied, 'she certainly is.' Dr Winter applauded particularly thunderously as Sequoia left the stage.

Ellie played a rolling fanfare on the piano and a boy's voice shouted out of the darkness, 'The great General, Julius Caesar has triumphed over his enemies and has returned home as a hero. But, oh dear! Not everyone welcomes his return.'

Clover couldn't suppress a smile as Josh strutted onto the stage, his thumbs hooked into his improvised toga as if he were stretching elasticated braces. 'Hello there everyone, I'm Julius but you can call me JC!' He waved informally towards the audience. 'I've just beaten Gnaeus Pompeius Magnus - better known as Pompey - but it was pretty hard work so I'm really ready for a rest now so that's why I've come back here, to sunny Rome!' Josh waved his arms around him, 'Phew, it's great to be back!' He looked around. 'Marcus Brutus, is that you?'

'Hiya Julius,' said Jake as he came on from the other side of the stage, 'Great to see you, it's been ages, did you have a nice holiday?'

'Well it wasn't exactly a holiday, you know?' replied Josh in the tone he usually used when he was contradicting his brother.

'Oh yeah, right, Pompey, well done for defeating him too,' said Jake.

'Thank you Marcus Brutus,' said Josh puffing himself up proudly. 'Now all I want to do is put my feet up and have a relax for a while thank you very much.'

Jake was getting into role too and now he eyed his brother warily. 'You say that but you're always on the go, aren't you? I bet you're not here for a rest at all. In fact, I bet you probably want to take over the whole city now that you're back. I mean, why wouldn't you, you make winning wars look so easy.'

'Well I am pretty great,' Josh conceded. Clover didn't remember them using exactly these words in the rehearsals but if they were improvising they seemed very sure of themselves so she didn't let herself worry about it. Josh continued merrily. 'Phew, I'm totally worn out, honestly you really don't have

27

anything to worry about, I've just come home to put my feet up for a bit, that's all there is to it.

'Alright,' said Jake (as Brutus). 'Where are you off to then?'

'Oh you know, popping down to the Senate, they've got some petition or something they want me to have a look at.'

'Umm, all right, I'll come with you if you want?'

'Brilliant yeah, you know we get along so well, it's almost like we're brothers.' This brought sniggers from the boys' classmates in the wings.

Josh clapped his hand on his brother's shoulder, 'Get off, don't be soft,' said Jake punching his brother on the arm. They had rehearsed that part of it but it had always been a mock-punch in rehearsals. This time, several members of the audience winced as they heard Jake's fist thump Josh's arm.' Jake saw the angry look in his brother's eye and made a dash for the edge of the stage. Josh lunged after him and tried to grapple him but he was too quick.

Sequoia spoke up from where she was standing near the piano, deftly drawing the audience's attention away from the potential violence while she narrated the next part of the action. 'Jealous of Caesar's power and scared that he might take over the city, the politicians in the Senate have decided to murder Julius so that he does not take over the city and rule it like an evil king.' She looked back towards the stage and the audience followed her gaze.

Josh staggered into the light, hastily splattered with red paint. This was not something that they could have practised in rehearsal without ruining their togas and Clover sighed as she noticed a lot of the paint had gone into Josh's hair. Clutching his chest and wheeling around Josh played the moment for comedy and he teetered from side to side, to the great amusement of his classmates. Jake came on after him carrying a ruler that had been wrapped in tin-foil to make it look like a dagger.

Josh whirled round to look at him. 'I cannot believe you did that Brutus! I'm really disappointed in you!' There were giggles from the audience as they spotted the updated version of *et tu Brute*. 'Why have you done this? What's your problem, are you jealous or something?'

'No!' snapped Josh, 'Well, not really, it's just that you're a bit *much*, you know? Not everyone wants to do what you say all the time.'

'But I wasn't even going to tell anyone to do anything anyway,' raged Josh, remembering at last to swoon from his supposedly fatal wounds. 'I just wanted a bit of peace and quiet now that I've finished all my war stuff.' Jake rushed up to catch him as he fell and managed it easily, lowering his brother to the ground.

'But you might have done something, mightn't you? You got too powerful and nobody could have stopped you on their own so everyone got together and decided to stop you for good. Say whatever you like but I think I did the right thing,' said Jake plaintively.

Josh, from a prone position reached out to the audience, 'Friends! Teachers! Parents! Listen to me for a moment.' He pointed at his brother, 'Don't listen to him, he totally murdered me,' Josh rolled his eyes while he mimed dying, dragging out his last breaths to make his plea to the audience. 'Even if he says he had a really good reason to do it, it doesn't make it the right...thing...to...do...'

'Or does it...?' said Jake, suavely pointing to the audience with both hands, dropping his brother to the floor as he did so with a triumphant shout of, 'You decide, people!'

The applause was very strong for them as they leapt to their feet bowing and beaming, but Clover was too surprised to clap, because just before the applause began, Mrs Chapman had sighed, rolled her eyes and whispered, '*Urgh*, heavens above, just kill me now!'

5

Clover felt increasingly unhappy at the thought of more criticism from Mrs Chapman, who actually groaned out loud during the kingless performance of the scene from King Lear by Olivia, Chloe and Holly. One particularly lengthy recitation from Olivia culminated in the words, 'My dear sisters, the two of you may have been denied your rights to our lands in France but think of poor me, who may no longer swim for fear of peasants seeing my magical tail.' This certainly was taking liberties with the original story. Clover winced as she heard Mrs Chapman shifting restlessly in the seat beside her. At least Dr Winter seemed to be enjoying the show.

'Our father must divide his kingdom evenly between us,' declared Holly as Goneril; Chloe's Regan added another plea for fairness. 'It is the only way. We must be just, so that England will remain strong,' she said earnestly.

Olivia turned on them both. Shakespeare's character study of quiet, modest Cordelia had been long forgotten and it was more than a little unclear where the story was going. 'Our kingdom faces many perils,' Olivia proclaimed in a shrill tone, 'but Britain must rule the waves or she will fall. That's why the only way to avert disaster is to contact my real father, Poseidon!'

Dr Winter let out a belly-laugh at this. Clover could not help but giggle too and the whole of the audience were soon entirely on board. Only Mrs Chapman sat in silence under a personal thundercloud that darkened exponentially as the interval arrived.

'Ladies and gentlemen,' said Bettina Williams as the last of the applause faded, 'if you would like to proceed through to the dining hall we will be serving a glass of wine to everyone of age, courtesy of the PTA.' This announcement received a round of applause of its own and Clover hoped that this might be her chance to escape back to her class.

But before she could move, she found herself engaged in conversation by Dr Winter. 'How do the children come up with these things?' he asked cheerily. 'They're so creative, what fun!' Clover looked wistfully towards her class in case they needed her but Ellie had jumped in to help organise them and waved Clover back with a signal that all was well. Clover sighed. Supervising the class had been her best excuse for escaping from the awkward spot between the two inspectors. 'A drink, I think,' declared Dr Winter, savouring the rhyme in the phrase and daring to peer around Clover towards Mrs Chapman. 'Something for you, Amanda?' he asked tentatively but with good humour.

'A measure of hemlock if there is one,' replied Mrs Chapman bitterly. Dr Winter's smile faded and it didn't escape

Clover's attention that quite a few heads were slowly turning in their direction. Mrs Chapman wasn't the slightest bit put out at the prospect of causing a scene. 'What do you expect from me, Arthur? I've always said that primary school drama was a waste of time. It should be done in amateur dramatics clubs after hours rather than in lessons.' Dr Winter started to reply but Mrs Chapman cut him off. 'Honestly, tell me you haven't seen exactly these scenes a thousand times before? Drama in primary schools simply means that the girls put on funny voices and the boys pretend to beat the living daylights out of each other.'

'Well, that sounds very much like Shakespeare to me,' countered Dr Winter trying to revive a sense of bonhomie.

'It isn't,' said Mrs Chapman rounding on Clover, 'you do understand that, don't you Miss Lightfoot, having perpetrated this naïve mangling of the classics on these poor children? Don't you see that what you've done here has nothing whatsoever to do with Shakespeare?'

'I...I...' Clover hesitated, finding herself at a loss for words. She could actually think of a number of quite sharp responses to such rude comments but she was keenly aware that Sequoia had slipped away from Ellie and was gazing at her through a gap in the crowd of adults. Clover searched for a response that would set a good example of how to deal with such a situation with dignity but she hesitated a fraction of a second too long and the moment passed.

'Oh for goodness' sake!' interrupted Dr Winter. 'You always were a dreadful pedant, Amanda, but now you are being ridiculous!' His voice carried easily across and, irritated, he spoke loudly enough for everyone in the hall to hear. 'Can't you see beyond your own petty theories of what ought to be taught? These children are showing an appreciation of the greatest works of English Literature and they are doing it at the age of nine and ten years old. If you had spent more time teaching rather than hiding in your office, then perhaps you would appreciate the challenges that such a feat entails.' Despite her respect for Dr Winter and the fact that he was obviously defending her, Clover felt extremely uncomfortable trapped in the middle of the argument.

Mrs Chapman's response was lightning-fast. 'I don't expect you to understand, Arthur. You've certainly never had what it takes to tell teachers when they should be working harder.'

'Whereas finding fault with everything is the only thing you seem capable of doing,' returned Dr Winter loudly. 'You pick holes in everything. It's typical...'

'Typical?' interrupted Mrs Chapman. 'You mean that it's typical behaviour for a woman, don't you? You never did respect anyone who wasn't a member of your old boys club.'

'Nonsense!' retorted Dr Winter, getting to his feet. 'If you had less of a chip on your shoulder about the disrespect paid to women in our profession then perhaps you'd spend less time insulting them yourself.' He glanced at Clover and lowered his voice as he tried to return to the facts of the matter. 'Miss Lightfoot shared her learning objectives with me regarding this performance and I find them to be exemplary. These children are engaging with the issues that Shakespeare was writing about. What could be more relevant?'

'This travesty of a performance has missed the point completely,' said Mrs Chapman. 'Shakespeare is all about the lyricism, the poetry, the legacy of the English language. But here, the words have been stripped bare. Where is the iambic pentameter?' She flapped her hand dismissively and Clover had to lean back to avoid being caught by her fingernails. 'I'm going to put an end to this kind of time-wasting once and for all. These children should be taught the basics of reading, writing and arithmetic to a good standard before they're allowed anywhere near Shakespeare and when they *are* taught about the classics, it should be done properly.'

Dr Winter looked irritated beyond all measure. 'You dare to lecture people about the sanctity of Shakespeare when you're the head philistine, planning to have teachers teach nothing but spelling and sums. Will you ban them from teaching art next? Or singing, will that be outlawed too?'

'You're being alarmist, *Dr* Winter. I'm simply talking about the careful regulating of what children are taught so that basic skills are given top priority. I suppose you would prefer the children to continue to spend all their time drawing pictures of dragons and drivelling about mermaids?'

'Oh you're going to regulate everything are you?' asked Dr Winter waving his hands in exasperation. 'Keep making more rules and everyone will eventually start to follow them, is that the idea, *Mrs* Chapman?'

'The idea, *Dr* Winter, is to cast a spotlight on schools such as this, which are so out of touch that the majority of what they teach is irrelevant nonsense. Once I expose their failings, the public and the press will ask how standards fell so low. Then I shall point to a certain regime of school inspection that merely showered schools with praise when they ought to have been giving out bad news and demanding improvements.'

Like an angered boar, Dr Winter dropped his brows and snarled in reply. 'My report on this school will be as fair and frank as always, make no mistake, I shall be very clear about every detail of anything that I find to be unsatisfactory.'

'Please, no,' squeaked Mr Fish meekly. He looked between the two of them in horror, realising that his nightmare of being condemned by both Inspectorates was materialising before his very eyes.

Mrs Chapman and Dr Winter turned on him as one, 'Please be quiet, Mr Fish,' they said in synchrony.

'I am going to prepare my formal report for the parents,' said Mrs Chapman huffily. She looked around at the astonished faces of the parent body and teaching staff. 'Some of us are bold enough to deliver the bad news in person.'

Dr Winter looked unsteady on his feet but he eyeballed his opponent fiercely. 'I shall also complete my report tonight and circulate it appropriately. I do believe you'll find that I am more than capable of delivering criticism when it is deserved.' With that he turned on his heel and made his way towards the PTA's proffered glass of wine. Mrs Chapman headed purposefully in the opposite direction, towards Mr Fish's office, which she had commandeered as her own.

Clover was left reeling in the middle of the hall, wondering whether a glass of wine might not be in order. However, the evening was still a long way from concluded and she had a premonition that she would need a clear head.

6

Turning her back on the wine and leaving the hall, Clover hurried back to her classroom to see what had become of the children. Ellie met her at the classroom door. 'What's going on?' she asked. Ellie's expression was a mixture of horror and excited delight; whatever was afoot, it was bound to be the source of wildly entertaining gossip.

'I'll tell you in a minute,' Clover said, too shaken to think beyond the practicalities of the moment. 'Is Sequoia with you?' she asked.

'I think so,' said Ellie, uncertainly. Together, they peered in through the small window in the classroom door but Sequoia couldn't be seen. 'I'm sure I saw her but I don't know where she went.'

'Don't worry just yet, I think I know where she is,' said Clover. She brushed past Ellie and went inside. Sequoia was exactly where Clover expected her to be. The girl was hidden in the den that Clover had constructed in the reading corner.

'Hey there,' whispered Clover, dropping to her knees to peer in at Sequoia. She spoke softly taking in the girl's nervousness. 'You're doing magnificently as the narrator, just carry on exactly as you were in the next half of the show and it will be amazing. Don't worry about the inspectors and their arguments. Their silly rows are nothing to do with us. We have a show to put on and you're an absolute star.' Sequoia nodded at this, finally managing a small smile. Clover rose to her feet once more. Leaving Sequoia to have some peace and quiet, she made her way back to Ellie who was standing by the classroom door.

'I didn't think to look for her in there. How is she?' asked Ellie.

'She's fine,' said Clover, 'She was still in the hall when things started to get nasty. Her mum often expresses herself by yelling, so Sequoia tends to think that everything's her fault.'

'If she's really alright in there, then you'd better spill the beans and tell me the whole story right now,' said Ellie, with a large grin on her face.

'Oh I can't bear to. Honestly, they should know better than to throw tantrums. The inspectors are like children fighting over their toys.'

'Are we one of their toys?' asked Ellie, struggling with the metaphor.

'I don't know, maybe the school is the sandpit that they're both playing in,' said Clover shaking her head. 'I get the feeling that they'd both like to make castles out of us or knock us down, depending on the game they happen to be playing.'

'It's a disgrace, honestly, the whole thing is turning into such a witch hunt,' said Ellie giving Clover's arm a squeeze. 'At least the children don't seem to be bothered by it.'

'Yes, it's just a storm in a teacup from their point of view, none of it matters really,' Clover replied, to reassure herself as much as her friend.

They were interrupted by Janet Clegg, who rounded the corner at speed and hurried towards them. 'Miss Lightfoot? Miss Robinson? Have you seen Mr Fish?' Janet called as she approached. She peered into the darkened classrooms as she came closer and glared through the windows that looked out over the playground but all she could see was her own reflection in the dark glass.

'He hasn't come this way,' said Ellie. What's going on?'

Once Janet was close enough to be sure she wouldn't be overheard, she hissed, 'We've got the parents' feedback meeting with Mrs Chapman right after the play and Simon's gone bloody AWOL.'

'Have you checked his office?' asked Clover.

'Of course I have but Mrs Chapman has locked herself in there and she won't come out,' said Janet.

'Gosh!' said Ellie, patently savouring the terrible drama of it all, although her voice remained carefully neutral. 'What's going to happen?' she asked innocently.

'We'll finish the show, of course,' said Clover firmly, feeling very strongly that she didn't have time to be amused by any of this.

'Quite right,' said Janet, recovering her poise. 'Miss Robinson, will you come and help me find Mr Fish? I need to talk to him before we meet the parents.'

'Oh, of course,' said Ellie, almost too eagerly, 'Tom Flint is around here somewhere, I can fetch him if you need more hands on deck.'

'I do,' said Janet. 'Would you fetch Tom and check the upstairs classrooms and the music room? I'm going to see if Mr Fish's car's still here.'

'He won't have just left, will he?' asked Clover.

'Simon was in a state, who knows what he's done?' said Janet. 'The parents are gossiping like mad, Dr Winter's taken a bottle of the PTA's best wine home with him and Sandy Delaney is properly on the warpath. She's talking about convening an emergency meeting of the board of governors and pulling Olivia out of school immediately.'

'I can see why Simon's so upset,' said Ellie soberly, 'I had no idea it was that bad.'

Her sympathy prompted Janet Clegg to rub her eyes. 'He's an idiot, I don't know why I bother.' Moved by a sudden sense that it was the right thing to do, Clover gave Janet a brief hug. The sturdy Mrs Clegg was so surprised that she accepted the gesture before she'd even realised what was happening. She gave Clover a grim smile, 'Thank you Miss Lightfoot. Miss Robinson, would you fetch Mr Flint and begin your search right away?'

Clover let them go and went back inside her classroom to be with the children again. As she entered she noticed that the children had become hushed and quite a few of them were staring at her, wondering what the fuss was about. She gathered them all together to settle them down, wondering how to explain it all to them.

'Let's start with a question,' she said. 'Who here has ever had a disagreement?' Every hand in the class was raised. She conducted a quick and efficient discussion about how easy it was to fall out with other people, even if neither of you were really in the wrong. A few minutes later the children were happily lined up again to return to the hall and continue the play. They looked confident once more and Clover felt a small sense of satisfaction about that.

The two seats on either side of Clover were unoccupied for the second half of the performance and she was heartily relieved not to be trapped between Dr Winter or Mrs Chapman again. Clover was still feeling the sting of Mrs Chapman's accusation that the play amounted to nothing more than the girls talking in funny voices and the boys beating the living daylights out of each other. She couldn't help but imagine the criticism that Mrs Chapman was planning to heap upon her and the rest of the school and she didn't like it one little bit.

Clover watched the rest of the show with an air of mild detachment. She observed that the children's interpretation of *A Midsummer Night's Dream* had been rather overtaken by the idea that people could be turned into donkeys. There was a common agreement in the small group of boys responsible for the scene, that many, if not all, of the challenges faced by Oberon, King of the Fairies, could be laid to rest by the wholesale transformation of inconvenient persons into mules. This treatment was summarily applied to all the principal characters of the play until a triumphant Oberon found himself the owner of a small herd. The only disadvantage in this scenario for Oberon was that the donkeys' notorious stubbornness required him to discipline them by unceremoniously kicking them on their rear ends. This, the boys had explained to Clover, was poetic justice that functioned on the much-discussed 'many levels of meaning' that she had urged them to explore.

Regretfully, violence and donkeys were also key themes of the next scene, which was based on Richard III. In this segment, King Richard's rhetorical battlefield promise, to offer his kingdom in exchange for a horse, was answered by the appearance of three magical donkeys, sent into the heat of the battle by King Oberon the Fairy, not as a gesture of regal solidarity but to quietly force a political settlement that would annex all the lands and territories of England, converting them into principalities of the *Land of Faerie*.

Clover found herself musing on the political astuteness of the boys' thinking and the subconscious legacy of British colonial history. She'd felt some misgivings about this scene but she had also endeavoured to support the children in exploring the story in their own way. Unfortunately, the outcome proved to be a minimally articulated portrayal of donkey-oriented carnage and swordplay, delivered in a style that owed more to Rowan Atkinson than Laurence Olivier.

The final scene of the show investigated the resolution of the problems that divided the star-crossed lovers, Romeo and Juliet. In the girl's version of events, the couple were helped by members of a benevolent coven of witches, who had lost interest in antagonising Macbeth. It emerged that the witches had discovered that being kind and friendly is altogether much more fun than torturing the inhabitants of Scottish castles or riddling in verse.

Clover barely noticed that the performance was coming to an end. She was still seeing everything through a haze of worry and confusion. Applause rang out around her and the audience members were already on their feet when she recovered a sense of where she was and what she was doing. Distracted by her thoughts, she smiled reflexively at the parents around her as the children in her class ran forwards into their loved ones' arms.

In the absence of Mr Fish, Clover stepped up to address the audience about the feedback meeting that was soon to take place. She knew that somebody needed to speak although she wasn't quite sure about what to say. But to her relief, just as the audience quietened, Janet Clegg appeared at the door and swept onto the makeshift stage to address the parents herself.

'Thank you so much everyone,' she said authoritatively, 'and thank you most of all to Miss Lightfoot's class for a highly entertaining evening. We will now adjourn for wine and nibbles until the inspection feedback meeting begins. We hope to see you all then.'

'Too right you will,' commented Sandy Delaney, which were menacing words indeed coming from the chairperson of the school's board of governors. Looking around at the assembled parents, Clover could see that the audience were already poised for a very different kind of theatre to take place.

7

Some of the children were taken home and others clung tiredly to their parents, but all of them had passed safely from Clover's sphere of responsibility back into their parents' care. Clover felt rather envious of those children who were heading home to their cosy beds. She could feel that she had very little to offer the forthcoming meeting and the whole enterprise appeared to be needlessly brutal. However, Clover mused, *needlessly brutal* seemed to be the order of the day when it came to school inspections.

The minutes dragged by and eventually Mrs Chapman emerged, striding imperiously from Mr Fish's office with her report in her hands. She walked indifferently past Ellie, Tom and even the ashen-faced Mr Fish who had been shepherded back to the hall by Janet Clegg. Clover couldn't help but notice that one of Mr Fish's cheeks looked redder than the other. Could Janet have slapped him to bring him back to his senses? Surely not, thought Clover.

Silence fell over the hall as the parents and staff filed back in. Bettina Williams slipped through the gathering with a Tupperware box full of donations for the school fund to lock up in the school safe. Many of the parents were still holding wine glasses and although some sat back down in the plastic chairs, most remained standing as if they were stoically preparing to meet their fate. Following her argument with Dr Winter, all eyes were firmly fixed on Mrs Chapman as parents and staff alike wondered just how bad her report on the school would be.

'Schools are all-knowing temples of perfection, are they not?' Mrs Chapman began. 'Who would dare to criticise them? Heaven forfend that anyone should utter the heresy that one or two of them might not be good enough. Imagine if the teaching staff present in this room took up a policy of never criticising the children, no matter what they did. How would the children know how to improve? Surely someone must do the difficult job of offering criticism, mustn't they?' Clover could see some heads around the room nodding at these words.

Mrs Chapman lifted her chin. 'That is why *I* am here. I am here to fight for your children's education. In that spirit, it is with a heavy heart that I must tell you that my report details this school's failure to provide the rigour and support that your children deserve. I am delivering these unwelcome words to you tonight so that your children will have the opportunity to benefit from the school's making improvements, so I urge you to think twice before shooting the bringer of bad tidings simply because you don't want to hear them.' Mr Fish leaned against the wall and seemed to be visibly shaking at the thought of the criticism to come. 'Therefore,' said Mrs Chapman, 'I shall now proceed to detail the school's failings and what should be done about them.'

'I think you should see this first,' said a firm voice from the direction of the school office. It was Bettina Williams, the head of the PTA with a sheaf of paper in her hands. 'This is a faxed copy of the report from Dr Winter, it's only just finished printing out.'

'Perhaps I should take that,' said Janet Clegg who was standing closest to Bettina.

'No, I don't think so,' said Bettina bluntly, 'I saw the first few lines as it was printing and I think everyone else should hear them too.' Nobody seemed to know whether they should stop her or not and so she stepped forward and read aloud.

'A crime has been committed tonight. The reputation of a fine school is being murdered before our very eyes by a vile woman who has set aside all reason for the purposes of dogma and personal gain.'

'He's absolutely lost his mind,' uttered Mrs Chapman, aghast. She started moving quickly towards Bettina with her eyes fixed on Dr Winter's report.

Bettina snatched it away from her and held it out of her reach. 'Don't you lay a finger on her,' snapped Sandy Delaney, her voice as vicious as a whip. Mrs Chapman, looked around and saw at once that the whole room was against her.

Bettina read out more from Dr Winter's report, 'Suffice it to say that all objectivity has been lost and not a word that Mrs

Amanda Chapman says should be believed. Over the time I have worked with her, she has revealed herself to be an entirely reprehensible human being and a creature capable of pure vindictiveness in a way that I had never imagined. I would urge you to take everything that she says with a hearty pinch of salt and make your own judgements about what is right,' Bettina finished reading, almost triumphantly. It was clear from the mood around the room that Mrs Chapman had won no friends during the time she had spent inspecting the school and she was met with cold, hard stares.

Mrs Chapman rounded on the parents, 'You believe that Dr Winter is your friend because he lives nearby, because he plays golf with you and implies that he will play favourites when the time comes. 'But he has fooled all of you. He is merely trying to save himself from his own lazy incompetence but the evidence is all on my side and you will soon recognise that all he has done here tonight is ruin himself.' she positively snarled as she turned on her heel and left. 'Murdered a school's reputation, I'll give him murder,' she said under her breath as she marched out of the hall.

Relieved to see her go but disoriented by the sudden turn of events, staff, parents and children looked to Mr Fish to make sense of what had taken place. Sadly, he was in no state to say anything at all and even Janet looked too flushed to comment. The meeting broke up in whispers and everyone started to make their way home. Exhausted, Clover slipped away too, realising as she did that the next school day would be starting again the very next morning. Little did she know what she would face when that hour came and how different a world the morning would bring.

PART II

8

The next morning Clover arrived to find what seemed like a very different school. The strange events of the night before seemed unimaginable in the light of day, as if they had been no more than a nightmare. She exchanged smiles with children in the corridors as they went around delivering the class registers and felt her mood lighten as they beamed up at her. There was an atmosphere of festivity in the classrooms that she passed as she made her way to her own room. The school had always been informal but today, with the ending of the inspection regime, it seemed that all bets were off. Board games and comics usually reserved for playtimes when it was too wet to go outside had been dumped on tables and boxes of scrap paper were being set out for children to doodle on.

She had already agreed to an impromptu team-teaching arrangement with Ellie and Tom that promised to give the children a bit of a special day and help all of the teachers play to their strengths. Tom Flint would run a rolling PE and games session on the field, which he loved to do. Despite his endearing lack of athletic talent, he always maintained that such things had nothing to do with being an excellent coach. Ellie had arranged a story writing class and Clover would be teaching watercolour painting. Maths and spelling could take a back seat for the day as the children had endured more than their fair share of lessons in basic skills during the last few weeks.

Clover arrived in her classroom and gazed out through the glass double doors into the playground where Tom Flint was already bounding about being encouraging in a tracksuit as a group of children helped him arrange the activities he was preparing. '*Hmm,*' said Clover to herself as she watched him running around with the children like a friendly dog playing with a litter of puppies.

She knew exactly how to set up her watercolour lesson for the different age groups that would come to her class throughout the day. It was a good job that she was starting with her own class though, because there was a lot of equipment to be cleaned and set up before anyone could begin. A trainee teacher in her class the previous term had been experimenting with tie-dye and batik, which appeared to be a diabolical means of making art using boiling wax. Several tables and chairs had been permanently marked by the experience and the children's creations were exactly what one would expect to find after nine year-olds had been systematically melting things.

There was a general air of saturnalian abandon and Clover reflected that even when the very worst things had been said and done, life went on regardless.

A rattling knock at her door startled her from her thoughts and she looked up to see Janet Clegg standing in the doorway, ashen-faced. 'Mrs Clegg,' said Clover looking around to see if any children were within earshot, 'Whatever is the matter?'

'You'll see,' said Janet. 'There's nothing to worry about at this point but I can't say more right now. Could you go to Mr Fish's office? You're needed there.'

'I've promised to run watercolour classes today with Mr Flint and Miss Robinson's classes.'

'I wouldn't give that second thought, Miss Lightfoot. Please leave that to me and make your way to Mr Fish's room at once. Everything will become clear, I promise.'

'Is he alright?' Clover asked, concerned by Janet's shocked appearance.

'Yes but it isn't Mr Fish who needs to talk to you.'

'Aren't you going to tell me what is going on?' asked Clover.

Janet sighed. 'It's far easier if he explains it to you himself, in fact it's essential. All will become clear and you have nothing to worry about but do hurry along now, you're expected.' Curiosity and confusion battled for supremacy in Clover's thoughts as Janet gave her an encouraging nod and sat down heavily in Clover's chair. She didn't look as if she were about to supervise a painting session. Clover left her to it, puzzled over why she would be needed. How bad could the consequences of a bad inspection be? What were they going to do, close the school? They'd have the parents to deal with first and that would be no small matter.

Passing the school office, the secretary, Mrs Clydesdale, was at her desk as usual. She offered Clover no more than grimace as she watched her pass. No doubt she was furious that someone had moved some tiny thing on her desk better to reach the fax machine. It was invariably some tiny slight that set Mrs Clydesdale on the warpath, a situation that could only be remedied by dedicating a portion of every staff meeting to addressing one or other of her grievances. She would sit grimly through each gathering until she was given the floor to ensure that the theft of half a packet of paper clips or the misplacement of her glue stick had been duly denounced. Then she would retreat back to her lair where, despite her gloomy outlook, she seemed to take care of all the actual budgeting and paying of bills that kept the school's lights on. Clover had taken note of her efficient approach but there was no way of thanking the woman for her dedication without arousing her eternally vigilant suspicions that she was being 'buttered up' for some forthcoming attempt to circumvent her authority. Clover gave her a respectful smile and was neither surprised nor disappointed when it was roundly ignored.

Mr Fish was quite informal in his habits and so the door of the head teacher's office usually stood ajar for visitors. In recent weeks, however, the door had been firmly closed as Mrs Chapman had taken over the office for the purpose of writing up her report for the Ofsted inspectorate. The door was closed again this morning and Clover had no idea whom she might find inside. She knocked gently and waited for a reply. 'Please, come in,' said a most unfamiliar voice.

Clover entered cautiously and found a most unfamiliar man standing close to the head teacher's desk in the small area that had been cleared of all Simon Fish's belongings and left empty for Mrs Chapman to use.

The man was staring at the display that had been put up above the desk. Undoubtedly it had been created by Mr Fish some weeks ago with the intention of influencing Mrs Chapman when she was using the room.

The display was entitled, 'Our wonderful, happy school,' and featured a photograph of a smiling Mr Fish, looking fit, well and bathed in holiday sunshine, his receding hairline bronzed by the sun. He looked genuinely happy in a way that Clover hadn't seen, ever, while he was at work.

Underneath the image of Mr Fish was a portrait of Janet Clegg, looking more like an author or a proud graduate in a photograph which had undoubtedly been taken professionally. She was sporting a fire-engine-red jacket with some padding at the shoulders and her jaw was set in a dignified manner that made clear that she would not tolerate fools gladly.

There was no picture of Tom Flint but he had hand-drawn a little sketch of himself as a stick man holding a sign saying 'Sorry I couldn't find you a picture in time.' Clover was featured next to a smiling Ellie at a birthday gathering held the previous year in a local Greek restaurant and there were even images of Bettina Williams and Sandy Delaney as the head of the PTA and Chair of Governors respectively.

Beneath the display, Simon had used bubble writing for the words 'We love our jobs so much!' To Clover, this seemed so on-the-nose that it might accidentally be construed as sarcastic. She knew right away though that it had been done in earnest. The whole display was the very representation of Simon pleading for the school not to be considered unkindly. Just how substantially this plea had been ignored by the inspectorate teams was now very clear to Clover.

The stranger flashed a grim smile towards her. 'Miss Lightfoot,' he said reaching back to tap at Clover's picture on the display. 'Thank you for coming to speak to me.' He was an older man in a crumpled black suit. He wore a sober, black tie but the top button of his shirt was undone. Though his face didn't look particularly old, he regarded Clover with the tired, sad eyes of contemplative bloodhound.

'Allow me to introduce myself. I am Detective Paul Meadows. I hope you don't mind if I ask you some questions?' He produced a small black wallet and he flipped it open to reveal a blue laminated badge inside featuring his own image.

'Would you please explain what's going on?' asked Clover feeling irrational flashes of guilt for crimes she could not even imagine.

'Absolutely, in good time, please take a seat. I need to ask you some questions.' Clover sat down, feeling rather numb. Her mind reeled as she prepared for whatever was to happen next.

'What do you know about the incident that took place last night?' he said unhurriedly.

'What incident?' asked Clover.

Detective Meadows shook his head. 'There was an incident last night but our procedure in cases like these is to ask a few questions before passing on any further information. We need you to help us give us a clear picture of what you saw and heard, if you would be so kind.' Clover nodded but the feeling of numbness and unreality grew stronger. 'Could you tell me in your own words anything you know about any incidents that took place last night.'

Clover took a deep breath. 'Well, there was a disagreement over the inspections that were taking place in the school. I...I got caught in the middle of it somehow.' Clover related the details of what had happened as the evening progressed. When she'd finished Meadows looked at her thoughtfully.

'Did you notice what time Mrs Chapman left?'

'I did, actually, It was 8.31pm exactly. I remember because some of the children were still there and I was contemplating how difficult it would be to teach them this morning.'

Detective Meadows frowned. 'Are you sure Mrs Chapman didn't leave earlier?'

'Quite certain, she was distressingly hard to ignore, in fact.'

'So I've heard. When Mrs Chapman did leave, did you happen to hear what she said to the group assembled in the school hall?'

Clover bit her lip. She only remembered fragments but those she recalled weren't flattering. 'It's a little bit of a blur but the gist was that she was intending to set things to rights.'

'You didn't hear her say that she planned on murdering Dr Winter?'

'Well, that was an expression she used but...what's happened?' Clover's blood ran cold. 'I refuse to answer any more questions until you let me know if everyone's alright.'

'Very well, that's quite understandable Miss Lightfoot. I'm sorry to have to inform you that Dr Winter was found dead last night at his home on Balfour Avenue, just a few minutes walk from here. It appears that the circumstances surrounding his death were suspicious to say the least.'

Clover felt almost too shocked to register anything at all. 'How did it happen?'

'It seems he struck his head upon an item of furniture.'

'What do you mean? Somebody hit him with a chair?'

Meadows sighed, 'It seems, from what we can tell, that he died from the impact of an award that he'd been presented with: a lifetime achievement award for his services to education.' Clover found herself too shocked to be immobilised by the situation. If there's one habit she'd gained from teaching it was that she'd learned not to be paralysed by the unexpected. Her thoughts returned quickly to the questions that she'd already been asked.

'Do you suspect that Mrs Chapman killed Dr Winter?' she asked, shocked by her own words.

'She is a suspect, certainly,' said Detective Meadows. 'She left a gathering with multiple witnesses making a statement to the effect that she intended to harm Dr Winter and she was then apprehended at the scene of the crime with blood literally on her hands.'

Clover blinked, trying to grasp the thought of Dr Winter being murdered. For a moment she thought she could hear his booming laughter and her eyes prickled with tears. She thought of Mrs Chapman sitting next to her in the darkness as they watched the play together. 'How did you catch her?' she asked. 'Did she turn herself in?'

Detective Meadows shifted in his seat, 'Well, she didn't resist arrest, which is not unusual when people are caught in the act but she didn't turn herself in. She actually claimed that she'd discovered Dr Winter in the condition that we found him, that being quite dead.'

Having played detective during dozens of playground disagreements Clover had the curious sense that something was not quite right about this story. 'I'm not sure I fully understand,' she said. 'How did you come to apprehend her at the scene if she didn't turn herself in? Who discovered the crime? How did the police come to be there at all?'

'It was a routine enquiry. A disturbance was reported at Dr Winter's house and a local constable was sent to see if he was alright.'

'Who made the call, one of his neighbours?'

Detective Meadows looked less comfortable, 'Well we don't actually know who called. They stated they were a neighbour but the call was made from a mobile telephone and we don't have any record of who it belongs to.'

'When was the call made?' asked Clover. 'If a disturbance at Dr Winter's house was reported before 8.31 then Mrs Chapman couldn't possibly have been responsible for it.'

Detective Meadows shook his head but he paused, blinking, even as he did so. Clearing his throat he flipped through his notebook and found a detail. He sniffed, rubbing his nose between his fingers. 'Well, it seems the call came in earlier, 8.08pm to be precise but it's only a few minutes' difference. Discrepancies do occur in these kinds of reports, especially when people unexpectedly find themselves in extreme situations.'

Clover looked at Meadows sharply. 'But if those times are correct then Mrs Chapman couldn't possibly have been responsible. At 8.08pm Mrs Chapman was two minutes away from starting her speech to all the parents. If you're doubting my recollection of that time, then look at the school newsletter. 8.30pm was the time when the inspection feedback meeting was due to start and that, at least, happened on schedule. If that's when a disturbance was reported then Mrs Chapman couldn't possibly have been responsible for it.'

Meadows looked thoughtful for a moment. 'Thank you, Miss Lightfoot, you've provided us with some valuable information and we'll follow up on it. Mrs Chapman isn't our only suspect, but I think we'll have to do some further checking before we rule her out.' Clover looked at him with concern, suddenly doubting his previous sense of certainty now that she saw him change his mind. Meadows was smart enough to notice her expression and he acknowledged her with a reluctant nod.

'You've been a great help, Miss Lightfoot and you may have even changed the direction of our enquiries. I must caution you, however, that if you talk to any of the other witnesses about anything that we've discussed then you might undermine their testimony and interfere with justice being done.'

Clover felt his reproof and gave him a respectful nod. 'I'll absolutely keep quiet about my observations from last night but I trust I don't have to refrain from talking to my colleagues completely.'

'No, not at all,' said Meadows. 'Everything here can continue as normal. The school isn't a crime scene and we don't want to upset the parent body any more than necessary. I'm sure it will be a shock when the incident is announced.' He looked down at his notebook. 'While I have you here, could I also ask you whether you've seen a Miss Antonia Reynolds, Dr Winter's deputy? We did question her briefly last night but we're having trouble locating her today.' Clover recalled Miss Reynolds smiling at her during her lesson feedback and shook her head. 'I haven't seen her around the school since early yesterday evening but you can't possibly suspect her, can you?'

'We don't make any of our suspicions public, Miss Lightfoot. We're just asking questions.'

'Antonia Reynolds was the last person who'd harm Dr Winter. You know she has been a close friend of his for years and he referred to her often and always very kindly.'

'Friendships, even close ones can turn sour and she would, of course, be the most likely candidate to replace Dr Winter in his role as Chief Inspector.'

Clover was incredulous. 'Are you suggesting she was seeking promotion by assassination? Oh please! Detective Meadows, do you really think that's in any way a likely scenario?'

'With respect Miss Lightfoot, I think that people are people and what seems small to one person might seem like a matter of life and death to someone else.' He shrugged, 'When things like that go too far, I'm the one who sees the consequences and, believe me, not everything that happens in real life is at all 'a likely scenario'. Many of them are far stranger than fiction. Anyhow, establishing the facts of where Miss Reynolds was last night will probably give us everything we need to clear her. That's something I can resolve as soon as we can locate her. Here's my card, do call me if you see her or if you recall anything further.'

Clover accepted Meadows' card and sat looking at it for a moment. 'Is that all?' she asked.

'That's all,' said Meadows in a reassuring tone, 'for now at least. Thank you again for your time and I am sorry to take you away from your class, Miss Lightfoot.'

'That's quite alright,' said Clover but she felt terribly sad as she rose to her feet. Poor Dr Winter's life had come to an end and that wasn't right at all.

9

As Clover began to wander back to her classroom, her surroundings suddenly seemed very alien to her. The joyful noises of the children's chatter and exclamations of glee in the background felt unusually precious.

Feeling rather dizzy, she stopped to steady herself beneath an enormous display featuring *The Twits*, the comically grotesque characters created by Roald Dahl. As the children's renditions of Mr and Mrs Twit leered down at her, she was struck by what it had felt like to be stuck between Mrs Chapman and the late Dr Winter as they'd been shouting at each other in the hall the previous evening. Clover tried casting Mrs Chapman and Dr Winter as the characters of Mr and Mrs Twit, two belligerent creatures, who were forever battling each other without any sign of redemptive qualities. Those caricatures didn't really fit them at all though: Dr Winter's protestations had obviously been intended to protect the school and her. How shocking and sad that he was gone. And surely Mrs Chapman couldn't be responsible for his murder, even if her heart were made of ice, she couldn't possibly have killed him. Clover shook all these thoughts away but before she could take another step, something caught her eye.

From the corridor window, she could see up to music room on the first floor. Her keen eyes picked out the figure of Antonia Roberts, Dr Winter's deputy, standing at the window: the very person that Detective Meadows had been asking about. Clover looked back towards the headteacher's office but the door stood wide open. Meadows had already left.

She turned Detective Meadows' card over in her hands and considered what to do for a moment before climbing the stairs up to the music room. She planned to pass the detective's card to Antonia Roberts and tell her to give him a call. He could take it from there.

The music room was used sporadically to say the least. Since the school didn't have a dedicated music teacher, the class teachers had responsibility for teaching music and whole-school singing took care of the rest. This meant that the music room was rarely used for teaching and had become a storeroom for a large collection of xylophones, each of which was inevitably missing several wooden bars. There was no shortage of claves, however, probably because the small wooden sticks were practically indestructible no matter what the children did to them. The room also boasted a box of broken drums and tambourines, the victims of over-enthusiastic percussion activity. A single black plastic clarinet with no reed and two broken valves stood like a lonely sentinel, watching over the lesser instruments from its expensive metal stand, which had endured the ravages of time more successfully than the clarinet itself.

To this disparate ménage, a host of non-musical teaching resources and curious follies had been added over the years. Few of them were ever used but each was considered too valuable or simply 'too lovely' to be thrown away. Most noticeable among these items was an enormous doll's house, made in the Victorian fashion by a parent or perhaps a local hobbyist. It was so enormous, cumbersome and fragile that there wasn't a way for more than one child to interact with it at a time without injuring it. To move it into a classroom would take up so much space that it would rob at least four children of the desks that they needed for their lessons. So resting in the music room the doll's house endured slow years of peaceful neglect, floating on the periphery of the school's consciousness in the hope of a time when it might be noticed again.

The humble music room was the base that the HMI inspectors had selected to use during their school inspection. It was much less of an imposition than taking over the head's office and, for the most part, the teachers had forgotten that anyone was using it at all. Clover knocked on the door and immediately heard Antonia's voice calling her inside. She walked in to see Antonia, red-eyed, attempting to force a smile.

'Oh, hello. I thought it might be one of the children,' said Antonia with some relief. 'They come up in twos or threes looking for music equipment. Sometimes they knock but usually they just wander in, ignore us completely and cart off a box full of wooden sticks like funny little workmen going about their business.'

'Yes, they can be very independent about fetching things,' said Clover, returning Antonia's smile with sympathy. 'I'm so sorry about what's happened,' she said gently.

'At least it is obvious to the police who is responsible,' said Antonia bitterly.

Clover thought carefully for a moment. 'We're not really supposed to talk about it but I don't think they're certain about anything yet.'

'Even if they happen to have caught a certain person with blood on their hands?' Antonia was certainly referring to Mrs Chapman. There had been a smouldering dislike between the two of them that had been apparent to anyone who had seen them together.

Clover shook her head but caught herself before she spoke again. She didn't know the details of what had happened when Mrs Chapman had been apprehended at Dr Winter's house. Perhaps she'd tried to give Dr Winter first aid and ended up covered in blood. Whatever had happened, the timing seemed to mean it wasn't possible for Mrs Chapman to be the murderer.

'The police are being very proper about it and they're not jumping to any conclusions,' Clover said, hoping that it was true. 'Anything might have happened. That's why I came looking for you, I saw you at the window and...' She was about to tell Antonia to call Detective Meadows when she saw what was on the desk in front of her. Clover stepped closer and looked at what Antonia was doing. Weighted at all four corners with loose wooden bars that had become separated from the xylophones was a curling, loosely furled fax machine printout. It looked like Dr Winter's report, the very same report that had caused such chaos at the parents' meeting the night before. 'What are you up to?' asked Clover peering at the printout curiously.

'Well, I'm trying to understand how this report was written,' said Antonia. 'I wasn't around last night, I had a personal engagement but when I arrived home I found a message on my answering machine telling me to call the police right away.' She closed her eyes for a second, as if pushing aside the painful memories. 'Of course I made a statement and then they told me what had happened.' She looked down at the papers before her again. 'It sounded like Dr Winter's report had caused a terrible stink at the meeting with the parents but I couldn't understand how that could be the case. So this morning I asked your school secretary about it and she gave me this.'

'That does look like the report I saw last night,' said Clover.

'But this report wasn't written by Dr Winter, or rather, he did write these words but he never intended them to go into a school inspection report, I'm certain of that.'

Clover looked puzzled, 'But how can you be so sure?'

'Because I've read these words before,' said Antonia, 'They're notes for a book Dr Winter wanted to publish after he retired. Did you know he was planning to retire this year? He only had a few months left before he was going to finally put it all down and then spend a few years taking train-spotting tours.'

Clover allowed herself a small smile at the thought of Dr Winter cheerfully train-spotting, but the expression faded immediately from her lips, 'No, I didn't know he was retiring. I'm sorry, Antonia.' She paused for a moment, 'Does that mean that you're going to take over as Chief Inspector of the HMIs?'

'I already have, practically speaking,' said Antonia, 'I was appointed as Dr Winter's successor two months ago and I'm doing the job in all but name. Dr Winter needed to stay on in his role for another four months to qualify for his pension, so we worked out a way of sharing the work until his official finishing date.' Antonia shook her head sadly, 'Dr Winter said that after he retired he was going to write a book to properly *set the cat among the pigeons*, as he put it. He didn't agree with the way that school inspections are changing and he wanted to give everyone a piece of his mind.'

'So the angry writing about Mrs Chapman in the report is really meant to go in Dr Winter's book instead?' asked Clover, looking again at the small typed print on the fax printout. 'You don't think he might have changed his mind and decided to share his thoughts in this report before he retired?'

'Like this?' asked Antonia, incredulously. 'Without the slightest thought of the consequences, hurling personal insults at an old colleague?' Antonia pointed at one of the paragraphs. 'He could write whatever he wanted when he retired but to put this kind of writing into a report about a school would be unthinkable.'

'So how did this end up being sent to the school?' asked Clover, she hesitated but then she said. 'You know he was drinking last night, don't you?'

'I know, and I know exactly what Dr Winter was like when he drank,' replied Antonia sharply, 'I worked with him for twenty years and if Dr Winter ever had too much to drink he became much more guarded. He was not a reckless man, quite the opposite: he'd never write a report after drinking.' Her eyes became bright with tears once more. 'He felt very strongly about things but he hated hurting people's feelings and he'd never do something as unprofessional as this.'

Clover nodded, taking a deep breath. She looked down at the report. 'So you believe someone else typed his notes into the report and sent it to the school.'

'They must have done,' said Antonia. She pointed at the other papers on the table. 'This is what should have been in the report,' she said, 'we'd been working on the draft together.' Clover's eyes sharpened as she read the words that were carefully typed on the other piece of paper. They had a completely different tone from the angry rant that was typed on the fax printout. The real inspection findings were cool and concise statements about the school, written plainly so that anyone could absorb them easily. It was far from good news. Dr

Winter's real report had pointed out quite a few things that might improve the way the school was run. Clover bit her lip as she read the criticisms. Her heart fluttered as she saw a mention of her own name but she started breathing again when she saw that the reference was quite complimentary. Still, she felt terrible for Simon and Janet. 'It's very different from the fax isn't it?' said Clover, soberly.

Clover looked at the difference between the report and the faxed copy. She knew she wasn't supposed to share her suspicions but there was nothing to stop her making observations about the evidence that other people were putting right in front of her eyes. 'You realise that whoever typed this report is almost certainly the person who murdered Dr Winter?' she said to Antonia. 'Who else knew about the things written in his notebook?'

'He kept his notebook at home on his desk,' said Antonia. 'I suppose whoever murdered him could have seen it and typed it into the report. Whoever it was, it must have been someone who wanted to ruin Dr Winter's reputation as well as end his life.'

'Or perhaps whoever did this simply wanted the school to get a better report and they saw the opportunity to try this,' Clover added uncomfortably.

'But who would care so much about an inspection report?' asked Antonia. 'I mean, they'd have to have lost all sense of proportion to be driven to murder someone over it.'

'Oh I think I know someone who fits that description,' said Clover, thinking of Mr Fish's disproportionate panic. She caught herself before she said any more. 'You should go and tell all of this to Detective Meadows. I imagine that as soon as you confirm your alibi for last night, he'll be entirely satisfied.'

Antonia gazed at Clover curiously, 'Do you have any idea about what really happened to Arthur?' she asked.

'I might have,' said Miss Lightfoot, 'but I've been told that it's important for me to keep my suspicions to myself and, of course, I could be very wrong indeed.'

10

Clover left the music room with the single thought in her mind. She had to have a word with Mr Fish. She felt sure that as soon as Detective Meadows managed to meet with Antonia he would shift his suspicions away from her and onto someone else. Clover suspected that when that happened, Simon would be the next suspect.

The toll of being the headteacher of a school visited by two inspectorates at once had meant that Simon had been acting rather erratically in the past few days. His behaviour had seemed even more strange last night and Clover realised that she'd formed a habit of mentally putting Mr Fish aside, as so many within the school community had often done. His opinion so rarely needed to be factored into any decision that it was easier not to consider him at all. At what point had he become so invisible?, Clover wondered. Faced with making a decision, he would find out what you wanted to hear and work his way around to telling you that, as if he had discovered it himself. Worse still, this answer was actually quite mutable. Mr Fish, true to his name, seemed to remember only the last conversation he'd had about any given subject, as if that definitive discussion wiped away all talk that preceded it. This could lead to cartoonish levels of misunderstanding where several different people could easily be absolutely certain that they had permission from Mr Fish to handle things in very different ways. The best way for such conundrums to be resolved was for Janet Clegg to simply declare what Mr Fish's actual position was, on the understanding that he would retrospectively agree with her or, at the very least, be so unsure of himself that he wouldn't challenge her on anything.

As she walked along, Clover asked herself whether Simon could have done something much more desperate than she had ever imagined. She would know once she saw him, she thought. Her meeting with Antonia Roberts had left her feeling quite sure of that. Antonia certainly wasn't guilty of killing her boss to gain power and Clover felt a terrible need to be able to tell herself that Simon Fish was innocent too.

Janet Clegg had said that he was taking some time to recover from last night, or words to that effect. She was covering for Simon, as she always did, but where could he be? Clover couldn't imagine but she knew whom to ask first.

'Excuse me, Mrs Clydesdale, could you tell me where Mr Fish is, please?' said Clover to the fearsome school secretary, in her most polite tone of voice.

'And what exactly does this pertain to, Miss Lightfoot?' asked Mrs Clydesdale, peering at Clover over her glasses. Clover was expecting to be challenged and stood ready to justify her request. She had already decided that it would certainly be easiest to tell the truth.

'I believe that he will shortly be questioned by Detective Meadows and I have an important matter to discuss with him before they meet.'

'I see, of course, Miss Lightfoot. To my knowledge, Mr Fish is on the premises. I believe he's working with a group of children, but I know not where,' she cocked her head to one side and beneath the armour of her formality Clover thought she could glimpse a trace of concern. 'I trust that nothing is afoot that requires the attention of this office?' she asked carefully.

'Not at all, Mrs Clydesdale, I believe Detective Meadows wants to speak to him, and I merely wish to advise Mr Fish so that he is not...' Clover searched for the right words, '...overly surprised.' What Clover meant was that she didn't want Simon to fly into one of his panics because Meadows had caught him unprepared. If that happened then poor Mr Fish might find himself under arrest simply because he was unable to explain himself coherently.

Mrs Clydesdale gave Clover a nod of understanding, a gesture of respect that few had ever received from her, and Clover hurried away. 'Thank you very much Mrs Clydesdale,' said Clover sincerely, almost bowing as she completed her transaction with the person who was the ultimate backstop for all of the school's business.

Many, many times Clover had used Mrs Clydesdale's legendary unapproachability to conclude difficult conversations about the minutiae of administration in the school. 'That sounds like something you'll have to take up with Mrs Clydesdale,' was a phrase that, once uttered, meant that the matter in question would probably vanish forever. Mrs Clydesdale's intimidating manner often made people think twice about whether they really wanted to pursue their question. Or, if they did find the need to bring their issue to her small, obsessively neat booth at the front of the school building, then the redoubtable Mrs Clydesdale would either provide what was required immediately or dismiss the matter with such summary judgement that it would never be spoken of again.

Clover's next job was to find Mr Fish. It was no coincidence that she went first to Ellie Robinson's classroom. Clover had noticed that the good Mr Fish had a certain affinity with her friend. It was something Clover would certainly never have mentioned to either of them; indeed, it was certainly no more than a certain level of shared understanding and although Simon was excessively mild and necessarily aloof when playing his part as headteacher, he was certainly quick enough to match Ellie's wits. If Mr Fish was looking for comfort then perhaps he would try to find it by spending some time with her.

Miss Lightfoot arrived to find Miss Robinson's class somewhat overpopulated. The seats and the carpet area were all full to overflowing with children, half of whom were from Clover's own class. 'Miss Lightfoot!' Ellie declared, beaming as the children turned around to look at her. 'We thought we might have lost you for the day,' Ellie said cheerfully, 'a few visitors from your class have come to join us in here.'.

'Ah,' said Clover seeing the familiar faces of Olivia, Holly, Chloe and Sequoia among the faces smiling back at her. 'Actually Mrs Clegg took over my class and I thought that she would teach the watercolour lessons I had planned but it seems that didn't happen.' Of course Janet didn't have time to spend the day organising painting and she must have worked out she could split Clover's class across the school, quickly taken the register and sent the children on their way. Janet had to be ruthless about using her time well but she did have a way of dumping things on people. This time it was Ellie and presumably Tom who had been landed with the extra responsibility of looking after groups from her class.

'Is everything alright?' asked Ellie innocently and all at once Clover realised that Ellie didn't know anything about the murder at all. Her heart sank as she felt the tiny gulf open up between them. She probably shouldn't let on about it at all in case Detective Meadows had some reason to interview Ellie.

'Here and now,' said Clover, 'everything looks absolutely fine to me. What are you all up to?'

'Well,' said Ellie engaging the children once more as she spoke in her most excited voice, 'we are all writing fairy stories. We've done one little exercise to invent the characters that we'll be using in our stories and now we're going to talk about the adventures that they might go on.'

Ellie loved to talk about stories and when she did this with the children they couldn't resist her enthusiasm.

'What makes something into a good story?' she asked the children with a smile, hands went up and Ellie started choosing responses.

'A story is just when something happens.'

'Something with a beginning, a middle and an end.'

'A story is about someone trying to get what they want,' said Olivia from Clover's class. She spoke up proudly, clearly thinking she had given the definitive answer. She looked surprised and suspicious when Ellie kept on taking alternative suggestions. After a few more ideas, Ellie picked up her pen.

'All of those things could be right,' she said, 'so let's try some of them out. Let's imagine that in my story I want to find this pen.' She held up the cheap red Biro.

'My story could go like this:

I want to find my pen. I looked around for it and I found it. I picked it up and put a tick on Olivia's book.'

Ellie flashed Olivia a quick smile to mollify her and draw her back into the discussion.

'Then I was happy because I'd found my pen.

So there it is,' said Ellie. 'I've got an amazing story haven't I? I bet everyone's going to love reading it.'

Something playful in her voice told the children that it was permissible to shout out at this point and a few of them hooted objections. Ellie pantomimed being confused.

'What are you saying about my lovely story? I think it's an amazing adventure. It's got all the things that a story needs, hasn't it? Something happens, it's got a beginning, a middle and an end, there's even something that someone wants. I think it's perfect. It could not possibly be improved.' She struck a pose of exaggerated superiority, her nose in the air.

Clover giggled and perched on one of the tables at the back of the classroom.

'No!' said a few of the children and even the quiet ones shook their heads with knowing smiles.

'Fine,' said Ellie. 'If you're all such experts on stories then how do we make my story better?'

'It could be a magic pen!' yelled Jake, unable to contain himself any longer.

Ellie took on his suggestion with a tiny gesture of warning, telling Jake to settle down a little bit.

'A magic pen, yes. Can someone put their hand up with a suggestion about what kind of magic you could do with my magic red pen?'

Sequoia was waving frantically and Ellie picked her out.

'When you put a tick next to something it could make the thing you ticked right, even if it was wrong and if you put a cross next to something you could make that thing wrong even if it's right,' said Sequoia.

This made Ellie laugh and she toyed with the idea appreciatively. 'That would definitely explain why I want to find my pen so much.' she said, 'I bet other people would probably quite like a pen like this too.'

More hands appeared with new ideas. 'Someone might take the magic pen because they wanted it for themselves,' said Josh. 'Because that way they could be the one who was right all the time, no matter what.'

'I see,' said Ellie. 'So who would want to be right so much that they'd steal my magic pen?' There were only a few hands up this time as the children thought this through. 'Yes, Holly?' asked Ellie, pointing to the quiet girl sitting next to Olivia.

'I think the Queen might want it so that she doesn't have to do what Parliament says any more,' said Holly seriously.

'What an interesting idea!' said Ellie, suspending her amusement carefully. 'So the Queen of England might sneak in and take my magic pen at break time. I have to admit, this is definitely sounding a bit more exciting than my first idea. Now, how am I going to get my magic pen back from the Queen?'

Hands were raised again and this time it was Chloe who spoke up from the other side of Olivia.

'You could write, "This magic pen belongs to Miss Robinson" on a piece of paper but you could fold it up so that the Queen can't see what it says, then when the Queen puts a tick on the paper it would make what you'd written true and that would make the pen yours again.'

'That's so clever!' said Ellie, letting her enjoyment of the idea spill out in her voice. 'I love the way that you tricked the villain into making a big mistake. That was really neat, I love it when stories work out in a neat way, don't you?' there was some authoritative nodding from many members of the class as they agreed that this was generally true.

'I also loved the way that you made the story into something really important. After you changed it, it wasn't just about a magic pen any more, it was about who has the power to say what's right and wrong. I think you've come up with a really amazing story!' said Ellie, her brow wrinkling as she thought through all the implications. 'For now can you work with your writing partner to think of ideas for making your own story into something that turns out to be really important. Let's see if you can come up with some ideas for that in the next fifteen minutes, shall we?' asked Ellie. With that, the class started to reshuffle themselves into seats where they could share their ideas.

Clover wandered through the swarm of children, smiling. 'That was interesting wasn't it?' said Ellie. 'A magic pen that gives you the power to decide what's right and what's wrong? Maybe that's all you need to be a school inspector.'

'That's what it feels like, doesn't it?' said Clover, 'The inspections weren't supposed to bother the children but when they see people with clipboards sitting at the back of the room, those things definitely filter through.'

Ellie shuddered, 'That Mrs Chapman has it in for me, you know.'

'I wouldn't worry about that,' said Clover, holding herself back from saying that there were more important things to worry about now. 'Have you seen Mr Fish anywhere?'

'I did see him out on the field, actually,' said Ellie. 'He was with Tom and he took a few of the children out of Tom's lesson to help him. Maybe he can tell you where they've gone.' Ellie looked out the window towards where Tom Flint was supervising dozens of children, all of them engaged in frenetic activities with coloured hoops, cones and beanbags.

'He's my next stop,' said Clover. Will you be alright to carry on with my lot for the rest of the morning? I'm not quite finished with...with the matter that Mrs Clegg asked me about,' said Clover. Ellie was going to be disappointed to discover that Clover had kept news of the murder from her but there wasn't anything that Clover could usefully tell her there and then.

'Oh yes, that's not a problem at all,' said Ellie happily, 'do whatever you need to do and leave these guys with me, I'll see you at lunchtime.'

'Thanks,' said Miss Lightfoot, gratefully. Ellie didn't know how much of a relief it was to have a little time to think and make sure she was doing the right thing. Clover was even more sure that a quick word with Mr Fish would settle her own mind and possibly save the poor man from a panic attack.

Being surrounded by normality let Clover breathe more easily again and she headed directly outside and across the playground towards the field. Tom Flint was supervising his class and more than half of Clover's class too, but he looked very much at ease. Tom had set them up working in small teams of three or four to create games of their own. The field was full of whoops and yells as tiny contests were resolved and replayed again.

'How do you get them to keep going?' Clover asked Tom as she approached. 'It looks exhausting.'

'I told them that they'll have to demonstrate the games they're inventing to the whole group in about five minutes. Knowing that they're going to put on a show adds a bit of friendly performance pressure so they're practising showing how the game works at the same time as exercising.'

'How did you get them working like this?' asked Clover, impressed.

Tom looked around the groups. 'The only rules are that they had to use throwing and running to create a game which could be played in twenty seconds. I also told them that the people watching have to be able to see if you've won or lost.'

Clover looked around. It was amazing how differently the different groups of children had responded to the same instructions. There were several variations on a simple game where players threw a small beanbag as far as they could and their opponent did the same, both players racing to fetch the object and race back to the start for a win. There were also elaborate variations where players had to climb through hoops, demolish tiny pyramids of cones or use their rivals for target practice. 'The trick is to isolate the actual skills you want them to repeat and get good at,' said Tom, 'in this case the running and the throwing. If you just play big traditional games then they might only get to kick a ball a few times before they decide that they're no good at it and refuse to join in.'

'It's really good work, Tom,' she said admiringly. 'You really know how to put yourself in their shoes, you know?'

'I wasn't sporty at school but I think I could have had a lot more fun in PE lessons if I'd learned enough basic skills. I'm just doing for them what I wish my teachers had done for me.'

Clover looked around at the groups. Some were aggressively challenging each other, while others were working more collaboratively and competing against a countdown. Everyone looked engaged and excited. 'I'm taking notes,' she said with a smile.

Tom looked shy for a moment, 'I'm sure there's not much I can teach you,' he said quietly.

'Oh?' asked Clover, not exactly fishing for compliments but pleasantly surprised by his words. 'I'm sure I don't know what you mean.'

'Well you're...amazing, you know that.'

Clover was slightly taken aback, 'I...I think you might be overstating that,' she said but she did feel a slight blush at his words.

'No, really,' said Tom. 'You're the one person Mrs Chapman and Ofsted couldn't find fault with,' he said. 'Really impressive.'

'Oh, you're thinking of Mrs Chapman?' said Clover, 'You didn't hear what she said about me last night did you?'

'No,' said Tom, 'but it couldn't have been too bad, could it? Nobody else managed to get away without something really spiky being said. Still. Anyway, it doesn't matter so much any more. Everything she's done is in question now that Dr Winter's finally taken her on.'

Mention of Dr Winter popped Clover's bubble and she felt the full weight of the situation pressing down on her once more. 'Tom, Ellie said that Mr Fish came out here to borrow a few helpers,' said Clover. 'Do you know where he is now?'

'Oh, yeah, sure,' said Tom. 'He's doing something in the domestic science room and he took a little gang with him to help out.'

'Did he seem...OK?' asked Clover.

'Yes, he actually seemed quite cheerful. Why?'

Clover was lost for words. She didn't want to lie to Tom but she wasn't sure what to say.

'Let's talk later,' she said.

'Sure,' said Tom, still looking puzzled as Clover walked briskly back towards the school buildings and headed for the domestic science room.

11

The domestic science room was a small temporary building that had come to feel very permanent. It had been put up in the late seventies at the far end of the playground where it was used for all kinds of things, with the sole exception of domestic science, for which it had become quite unsuitable. The room contained two immaculately maintained but unusable ovens, a broken sewing machine, which had been kept for the purpose of demonstrating how a sewing machine could be taken apart and reassembled, and an industrial lathe that had been donated to the school in the last will and testament of a local enthusiast. The lathe had been kept because of its reputedly tremendous resale value. This made perfect sense, except that there had been a problem with the will, meaning that the lathe had been suspended in a legal limbo that prevented it from being used, sold, removed or even touched. However, the lathe did look very fine and serious and it was a matter of great pride for Mr Fish that children would sketch it while being lectured on how it might have been used for all manner of heavy industry such as turning chair-legs and milling decorative pieces of bannister. The ovens were free of legal restrictions but had been untouched for years due to a problem with the electricity supply which might, at any moment, decide to shut itself off for its own mysterious reasons. The room itself, however, was quite impressive to look at and, as Mr Fish pointed out regularly in staff meetings, it was always most educative to disassemble the sewing machine and look at how it had once worked.

Clover hadn't visited the domestic science room for at least a year but, as she approached, she could see a bustle of activity. Mr Fish and a busy cadre of eight children were hard at work at a large table. Everyone's attention was focused on an enormous banner, at least three metres long, lolling off each end of the table. Clover was reminded of the Bayeux Tapestry, however, instead of describing the Norman Conquest, Mr Fish's black sugar paper equivalent was a collage of drawings and notes about the school. These were being created and assembled under an enormous heading in flamboyant bubble writing that read, Our *Inspection Success*!

As if he could read the historical allegory in Clover's mind Mr Fish stepped up alongside her and declared, 'History is written by the victors, eh?'

Beneath the heading were pictures and quotes that had been copied by the children in their best handwriting, cut out and stuck onto the sugar paper in a more or less even distribution across the whole of the surface. There was a production line at work, starting with a huge pile of papers for words and phrases that had been highlighted by Mr Fish. The children were choosing phrases and copying them onto coloured paper;

drawing a cartoon or picture to match the quote (although some of these were wildly missing the point) and the final output was being quickly glued into place.

'What are you doing, Mr Fish?' asked Clover, slightly alarmed by the pace of what she saw.

'I'm presenting the outcome of our recent inspections graphically for the benefit of the parents and the staff. I think if we place this strategically in the entrance hall then we'll really get our message across.'

'You don't think that you're somewhat selective with the information that's being presented here?' asked Clover.

'Absolutely,' said Simon. 'It's always good to be positive and I've made it clear that these are only the positive aspects of the inspection outcomes.'

'Where have you done that?' asked Clover sceptically.

'In the title, you see, this is a banner to celebrate the successes of our inspection.'

'So are you going to make another banner for our failures?' asked Clover in a tone that allowed a little incredulity to spill out. Two of the children glanced up at her before turning back to their work.

Mr Fish turned to face Clover. 'Miss Lightfoot, as headteacher I must make the difficult decisions about what we communicate to others and what we work on internally. I've made that decision and I shall stand by it.

'Mr Fish, do you recall the events of last night? And the things that Mrs Chapman said in front of the parents?'

'Oh yes, of course, but since Dr Winter disputed her position I feel confident that nobody will pay her much heed.'

'You do know,' said Clover hesitatingly, 'that Dr Winter is no longer able to *actively* dispute Mrs Chapman's position?'

'Yes,' said Mr Fish nodding soberly, 'I was informed of that.'

He glanced around at the children and deftly continued the conversation on the subject of Dr Winter's untimely demise in such a way that the children were unlikely to grasp what was going on.

'My understanding is that Dr Winter's *inactivity* is related to Mrs Chapman's *initiative*.' He shook his head and shrugged, 'It seems to me that this all but sets the recently, um, *deactivated*, Dr Winter's words in stone, does it not?'

'I'm afraid that, far from being set in stone, his words may not even have been correctly set down on paper!' said Clover.

'What do you mean by that, Miss Lightfoot?' asked Mr Fish, suddenly alarmed. Having taken a step too far, Clover was suddenly keenly aware of how much she couldn't say. She had only wanted to talk to Mr Fish to make sure he wasn't cowering in a corner unable to string a sentence together. Finding him practically celebrating was distasteful to say the least.

'All I can say is that it seems very little has been settled and it might not be wise to write your version of history just yet.' She examined Simon thoughtfully, thinking of the questions that Meadows would be sure to ask him. 'Where were you during the second half of the performance last night?' she asked.

'Miss Lightfoot, as headteacher I cannot always attend every school gathering, I had some urgent business that demanded my attention and I'm afraid the matter simply couldn't wait.'

'That's good to know,' said Clover, 'because whoever you were conducting your urgent business with will need to vouch for where you were in the time between the argument and Dr Winter's, *conclusion.*'

'But I don't see that it matters! Surely Dr Winter's *departure* occurred much later in the evening, after he sent that tremendous fax that defended our reputation?'

Clover shook her head, 'I wouldn't take anything for granted just yet,' she said. 'Where exactly did you go for the important school business?'

Simon's face fell but he tried to keep his voice merry as he replied, 'Well, um, it was in the best interests of the school for me to compose myself to prepare for the meeting later on. I'd volunteered the use of my office to Mrs Chapman so I took the opportunity to undertake a walking meditation, of the kind that we were trained in so successfully during our in-service staff training.'

Clover did recall the session he was referring to; as it happened, she recalled it all too well. The walking-meditation had been a passing recommendation from a tough-talking teaching consultant who had impressed Simon at a headteacher's conference. The man, Clover didn't recall his name, had been invited by Simon to attend a staff meeting, not realising that Simon intended to entrap the poor visitor into leading the meeting himself. Flustered and increasingly belligerent as he realised he had been tricked into running the meeting for free, the consultant described a 'walking meditation that could be used to *reset the perspective of the whole staff about the curriculum.*' At that point he'd led the entire group outside and invited them to silently contemplate their own walking whilst exploring quiet areas of the school they might otherwise never see. While they were doing that, he walked as far as his car, discovering at that moment, that he had an unexpected appointment that he needed to attend to.

Though it had been apparent at the time that there was some level of deception involved in these actions, the staff as a whole had taken pity on Simon and praised the experience to save his blushes. Socially, this had seemed like the only possible course of action. However, Simon, who was always thirsty for praise of any kind, had rewritten history in his own mind to enshrine this session as one of his greatest achievements as a headteacher, coming eventually to believe that a key feature of his leadership had been providing a marvellous, refreshingly innovative and entirely free walking-meditation workshop. It was by means of this painfully maintained fiction that *going on a walking-meditation* had become shorthand for Mr Fish absenting himself from proceedings he couldn't cope with.

Clover shook her head firmly. As an explanation, a solitary walking-meditation really wouldn't do in the current context.

Noticing the lack of acceptance in Clover's expression, Simon shook his head questioningly, 'No?' he asked.

'No!' said Clover, setting niceties aside. 'I think you should try to remember exactly where you went when you left the hall last night.' Mr Fish blanched as he thought through what this might mean.

'You can't imagine there would be any question of me actually being responsible for Dr Winter's *departure*?'

'If I were you, I would make sure that I was prepared to answer questions about where you were and when, that's all,' said Clover compassionately as she saw Simon's hands tremble. She mused that it wasn't his fault that he'd ended up in this position but with Simon it seemed that was always the case. She doubted he ever wanted to be a headteacher. But in some schools it was all too easy to tumble upwards through the ranks and end up stuck in a role you had no desire to occupy. To Clover, Simon's seemingly Machiavellian, penny-pinching ways always seemed to be an expression of an essential lack of confidence. Poor Mr Fish, forever in a tight spot, would invariably attempt to claw back a little dignity or a little money at the worst possible time and in the worst possible way, not because of poor moral standards but simply because he couldn't take it any more. Being a headteacher and thus responsible for everything was a position Clover didn't envy in the least.

They were interrupted by a sharp knock at the door. Mr Fish froze, though the children continued industriously, quite indifferent to the world of adults. The door opened to reveal the tall figure of Detective Meadows. Simon did his best not to squirm and he put on his most authoritative voice. 'Detective Meadows, I take it there's more we need to discuss,' he said briskly. 'Take over here for me will you Miss Lightfoot?' he said in a businesslike way but as he left, he gave Clover a silent look of thanks.

Meadows stood in the doorway. 'Having a busy morning, Miss Lightfoot?' he asked.

'Not as busy as you, I imagine, Detective Meadows.'

'Oh I don't know,' said Meadows, turning away, 'I don't know about that at all.'

It was almost time for lunch and Clover called a halt to the work on Mr Fish's banner, sending the children to the cloakroom to fetch their coats. She shook her head. Many of the phrases were taken from sections of the false report that had been sent in after Dr Winter's murder.

'An exceptional school recognises that all people are exceptional in some way.' That seemed like a very general statement rather than praise for this school in particular.

'When an institution provokes teachers to have vibrant opinions on the school's policies, then this is an exceptional school indeed,' read another quote. Again, this didn't sound at all familiar. School policies were usually only written down to try to codify some common-sense procedure that had evolved from necessity. There weren't many opinions voiced about them in meetings that Clover had ever attended, vibrant or otherwise. Not knowing what to do with the banner, she left it where it was. She saw that the room was reasonably tidy and then she made her way to the staffroom for lunch.

12

The bell rang for lunch and torrents of children were released into the playground. They had no shortage of energy even though the teachers that came to see them out looked variously exhausted and bedraggled. It had been a hard few weeks for the staff and they were taking the chance to cut some corners now that the spotlight had moved away from them.

Clover smiled. The staffroom would be full of cake. There was often cake in the staffroom. In fact there were very few days when cake didn't appear. Teachers, like bees, would hum by at various points during the day to take a sip of nectar from a common sugary source blooming upon the staffroom table. Any excuse for providing cake was deemed valid and reasons ranged from birthdays to minor domestic events like someone doing a 'big shop' and finding room in the boot of their car for a selection of cake from the reduced aisle of the supermarket. Last night had seen the end of the inspections and the performance of the play, so already there were two good reasons for an abundance of cake.

The school moved to a subtle rhythm of its own whereby knowledge about peaks and troughs of activity passed by osmosis through the entire institution. A class teacher preparing to undertake some kind of challenge, such as the production of a play would, without ever requesting it, be provided with a certain amount of grace by the other teachers. They might find themselves offered all manner of tiny degrees of support to acknowledge their extra effort. This might be as little a thing as teachers holding back their classes in the corridor so that others could go into assembly without having to wait. Or more generous support might be provided by sharing scarce resources with a class carrying the particular burden. These tiny acts of mercy quietly acknowledged the extra effort being made. It was in this spirit that Tom and Ellie had taken the children from Clover's class that morning without the slightest complaint. Correspondingly, Clover had little doubt that the pressures of the inspections on everyone would have resulted in a record deposit of cake in the staffroom that day, even if only a few staff members knew what had happened the night before by this point in time.

Clover let herself into the staffroom and was met by an icy silence. She scanned the room. There was certainly an abundance of cake on the table and that, she thought, was the most important thing right now. Icing glistened on a gorgeous-looking, home-made lemon drizzle cake in the shape of a giant ring. But behind that, on a glass cake stand, was a majestic gateau. This had obviously been purchased as a treat from the nearby French patisserie that was only visited on very special occasions. The gateau resembled a chocolate castle with crenelations of chocolate cream and thin shards of curled chocolate rippling like flags on top. Raspberries, strawberries and blackberries tumbled over its sides, covering the chocolate topping that was undoubtedly hiding beneath.

There were several members of staff standing around the room and they appeared to be staring at Clover. Confused, but imagining that some kind of joke was being played on her, she stood still, looking questioningly at her colleagues before realising that they were all looking at the figure sitting in the chair beside the door.

It was Mrs Chapman. That explained the silence and frosty expressions on their faces. Tom and Ellie hadn't arrived yet and Clover felt the urge to turn back outside to warn them. Mrs Chapman had seated herself so she would overhear whatever conversation was taking place between teachers as they entered the staffroom. She raised an eyebrow as she looked up at Clover before returning to the notes she was writing on the clipboard in front of her.

Clover stepped out of the way as the door opened behind her and Janet Clegg came in, eyes wide at the table full of cake. She spoke up loudly, 'Goodness me, what are you all waiting for?

The enemy are no longer at the gates. I expected to see decadent degrees of consumption taking place in here.' Miss Lightfoot sighed and put a hand on her shoulder but it was too late.

'I hope you don't regard *me* as *the enemy*, Mrs Clegg,' said Mrs Chapman coldly. 'For my part I rather respected your forthrightness in actually getting things done.'

Janet turned to see Mrs Chapman with her clipboard and stumbled an apology. 'Why, Mrs Chapman, I do beg your pardon, I didn't think I'd see you again for quite some time.'

'Well that much is abundantly clear,' replied Mrs Chapman with a swift tick on her clipboard, as if there was a box there that should be checked whenever she had succeeded in catching someone out. 'At any rate, I have decided to extend the inspection of this school for a few more days in order to make sure my report properly reflects what is really going on here.'

Now wait a minute,' said Mrs Clegg. 'The inspections have been concluded and if you have any plans to follow up with more visits to our school then you will need to discuss this matter with me and Mr Fish.'

'Oh I promise I shall be having many discussions with you both but I don't think you're going to like them very much. If you found my report last night to be distressingly honest then I have to tell you it's nothing at all compared to the report that I intend to issue after the things I've seen today; whole classes doing nothing but playing games and writing random stories. I've seen groups making hats and paper chains as if they didn't have a care in the world.'

'Surely, you understand,' said Clover feeling a need to defend everyone, 'that the school has been working in a very intense way for some time to provide the inspectors with every opportunity to see us working well. It's only natural that we should slow down a little. Any school would do the same.'

'Miss Lightfoot, what I understand is that a school which already seemed lax and lazy to me was simply putting on a performance to disguise an even more indolent disposition,' said Mrs Chapman, 'one that I have now begun to document most thoroughly and will report on accordingly.'

'Under the current dreadful circumstances, how could that possibly be fair?' asked Janet Clegg. Although she couldn't state her objection out loud, Clover understood her implication. Dr Winter had died less than twenty-four hours ago. How could Mrs Chapman possibly hope to continue her inspection of the school at a time like this?

'It seems perfectly fair to me,' snapped Mrs Chapman. 'After all, you're still teaching, so there's nothing to stop me inspecting your teaching, is there?'

She seemed very angry. Perhaps it was the trauma of Dr Winter's death that had done this to her, thought Clover. Mrs Chapman must have spent some of the previous night talking to the police while being under suspicion of Dr Winter's murder. In view of that, Clover was inclined to try to be more understanding of Mrs Chapman's rage. It must have been a nightmare for her, thought Clover, reflecting on the rumours she'd heard of Mrs Chapman literally having blood on her hands. Despite her anger, Clover tried to withhold her judgement, at least until she knew more about what had happened.

'I am calling a special staff meeting later today to communicate some serious news for those who haven't yet been informed,' continued Mrs Chapman. 'I also intend to discuss how the dreadful events of last night are to be communicated to the parents.' Janet Clegg looked as if she might challenge Mrs Chapman on calling a staff meeting, something that was really only in the power of Mr Fish or herself, but the way Mrs Chapman had declared her intention seemed deliberately provocative, as if she hoped Janet would say something so that she could undermine her further. 'I look forward to seeing you all there. Please, do go ahead and enjoy your cake.'

There was some puzzlement on the faces of those who still didn't know that Dr Winter had been murdered, but Janet Clegg looked quietly furious and a little bit scared. Disturbed by the whole encounter, Clover was almost too upset to take a large slice of gateau before she left to find Ellie.

13

As she left the staffroom at speed, carefully protecting the cake from any passing children, Clover found Ellie in the corridor outside. 'Miss Robinson,' said Clover, turning Ellie around and directing her back towards her classroom. 'We really must talk.'

'But...cake!' squeaked Ellie plaintively.

'I've brought you an extra large slice,' said Clover, 'I'm afraid I don't feel much like having any myself any more.'

'Why on earth not? Clover, what's going on?' Ellie looked at her seriously.

'Right now, Mrs Chapman from Ofsted has planted herself in our staffroom and she's making notes on everything, preparing to wreak her revenge on everyone for the damage done to her reputation last night. But that isn't even the half of it, we have to talk, I have to talk to someone.'

'Oh, gosh, alright,' said Ellie and let herself be carried along by Clover towards her room.

Once the door was safely closed behind them Clover thought about what she was allowed to say. She wasn't about to break any rules but she certainly knew how to bend them when something absolutely needed to be done and this was one of those times. Clover certainly wasn't going to tell Ellie anything about Dr Winter's death but she could certainly tell her enough to help her guess.

'Ellie, I'd like your opinion on a story that I'm writing with my class.' If there had been anything normal about this conversation Clover would have been much more chatty about it, as it was, this request was delivered with deadly seriousness and Ellie read at once from Clover's actions that something was dreadfully wrong.

'I'm listening,' she said carefully, 'tell me the story.'

'Well, it takes place in a wood,' said Clover opening her hands to gesture to the school around them. 'It's a perfectly ordinary wood and there are dozens, in fact, there are hundreds of woods just like it all over the country.'

'Yes, I see,' said Ellie picking up Clover's meaning at once as she unfolded the napkin that Clover had used to grab the slice of cake. There were indeed layers of chocolate sauce in between the sponge, Clover noticed, before she remembered that she'd lost her appetite.

'So there's this wood and it's full of woodland creatures. There are some perfectly lovely bunnies in the wood, for example,' said Clover waving her hand between the two of them.

'Right,' said Ellie, understanding and trustingly following along.

'There's also a fish who lives in a very small pond in the middle of the wood and he actually thinks that he's the king of the wood.'

Ellie nodded, 'Because when any of the animals go to see the fish they always call him, *your majesty*, even though they never really do any of the things he says. The fish doesn't even realise because he stays in his little pond all the time,' said Ellie, checking that she had grasped what Clover was telling her.

'Exactly,' said Clover with a smile, 'you can't really blame the fish for who he is though, he'd just flop about and die if he actually jumped out of his pool and started trying to rule the wood, it's just not in his nature. But you've got my meaning exactly. Your comprehension skills are fantastic by the way.'

'Why thank you,' said Ellie making a playful curtsey. Clover bit her lip, and for a moment she hesitated about burdening Ellie with the whole of the story even though she had planned to tell her in such a way that they wouldn't get found out. Clover despised gossip and she was only prepared to talk like this to Ellie because she needed a friend so desperately just then.

Clover took a deep breath and plunged ahead.

'So everything's usually peaceful in the wood but suddenly two packs of foxes come along,' said Clover. 'One pack is led by an old fox who's well known to the bunnies, the other woodland creatures and even the fish. He seems quite friendly and he even lives in a local den, but he's still a fox and sometimes he has to eat other woodland creatures to stay alive, whether he likes it or not.' Clover watched Ellie to see if she was keeping up and Ellie nodded, amused. She couldn't miss such an obvious allusion to Dr Winter and his HMI team of inspectors and they were certainly capable of savaging someone's reputation from time to time.

'But one day, a rival pack of foxes arrive in the wood. This new pack of foxes is led by a little fox who is clearly much hungrier than any of the older, larger foxes.' Clover thought of the feral gleam she'd seen in Mrs Chapman's eye as she talked about her Ofsted inspectors. 'She's got a brand new pack and she's gradually moving in on the old pack's territory. So the two packs of foxes are prowling around the wood, thinking mostly about each other but also looking for any animals that are weak, to eat them first.'

'I'm not sure I like the idea of this story so much when you put it like that,' said Ellie, looking glum. 'It really seems like someone's about to get eaten rather nastily, is that how the story ends?' Clover could see that Ellie was thinking along the right lines but she could also see that her friend was still thinking of nothing worse than a bad inspection report and Clover had to get her to see that it was really much worse than that.

'Suppose that the old fox, who's in charge of one of the packs of foxes, quite suddenly, literally, actually, dies,' said Clover, 'in the most suspicious circumstances possible.'

'What?' said Ellie, startled, crumbs of gateau falling from her lips.

'I mean exactly what I say, the old fox is found one morning, quite dead,' said Clover. She felt a fresh wave of sadness despite the ridiculousness of having to wrap up the news in a foolish story. 'He was knocked on the head with his own, um, rabbit catching award.'

'What?' gasped Ellie, confused for a moment as the metaphors became mixed up with reality.

'The details aren't really that important, except to say that the old fox died violently and somewhat ironically,' said Clover, 'and it is clear it wasn't an accident.'

Ellie absorbed this news slowly.

'That is quite shocking,' she said, at last. 'It doesn't sound like the kind of thing that usually takes place in this kind of wood.'

'It really isn't,' Clover agreed.

'Why is everyone keeping it a secret?' asked Ellie.

'Well,' said Clover, 'when the old fox got killed, a big bad wolf came sniffing around and he's nosing about, trying to decide who did it so he can eat them up. He doesn't want any of the woodland creatures to know he's there until he's picked out the culprit.'

'A wolf?' asked Ellie.

'A very properly authoritative wolf,' said Clover thinking of Detective Meadows. 'The kind who normally turns up when blood has been spilt but a creature who is certainly used to dangerous and difficult hunting.'

'Who do you think really killed the old fox?' asked Ellie, troubled by the thought as she contemplated the reality of the situation.

'It's just a story, Ellie,' Clover reminded her, 'I haven't got the slightest bit of school gossip to pass on, you know I never gossip.'

'It's true, you're usually very boring like that,' said Ellie, cheekily. 'But in the story, who do you think really killed the old fox?'

'Well, at first the wolf thought that it was the little fox who'd killed the old fox because she wanted to take over both packs but it turns out the little fox couldn't have done it. She was definitely somewhere else at the time.'

'Let me guess,' said Ellie grimly. 'The little fox was attending a party put on for her by the woodland creatures, in the hope that she'd decide not to eat them after all.'

Clover smiled with relief at being understood. 'Yes, that's exactly where the little fox was and it definitely couldn't have been her. So the wolf has started to think that the fish must be responsible, despite the fact that he seems too scared to even get out of his little pond.'

'The fish? No, surely not.'

'That's exactly what I was thinking too but a lot of stories have twists that you can't possibly predict, isn't that right?'

'I suppose it is,' said Ellie, 'you can see that the fish might want the foxes to leave the wood but he couldn't have been the only woodland creature who felt like that. What about his sidekick, the prickly hedgehog?'

'The prickly hedgehog?' asked Clover.

'The hedgehog who really makes everything happen in the wood, you know, the power behind the throne. She would be at least as motivated as the fish to get the foxes under control.' Clover nodded thoughtfully as she realised that Ellie was talking about Janet Clegg.

'I hadn't thought of that.' said Clover. 'The hedgehog was unaccounted for at the time of the murder. She was running around looking for the missing fish when it happened and she wasn't the only one.'

'Who else? I mean, which of the other woodland creatures weren't at the party?' asked Ellie, sharply. 'That's where we have to start if we're going to work this out.'

Clover hesitated as she realised who else was unaccounted for, 'The clever little owl,' she said. 'He wasn't there at the party either, or he might have turned up late to it, at least I don't remember seeing him.'

'Who's the clever little owl?' asked Ellie, breaking out of the story euphemisms briefly. 'You don't mean Tom Flint?'

'I mean the clever little owl who seems completely sweet and kind and is good at solving everyone's problems,' said Clover, confirming Ellie's guess with a nod. She let the thought sink in for a moment. 'I don't want to think that he could do something this awful either but I don't want to think that any of the woodland creatures could have done this. And the big bad wolf has almost bitten the wrong creature's head off by accident once already and I want to make sure that doesn't happen again.'

Ellie took Clover's hand, 'As I see it, all we can do as happy little bunnies is keep hopping along and see if there's anything we can find out that will help the truth come to light.'

'Thank you, yes, my thoughts exactly,' said Clover breathing a sigh of relief. She went back to her own classroom and fetched her sandwiches from her bag before thinking through the questions that were playing on her mind.

The bell rang for the end of lunchtime and Miss Lightfoot was the picture of decorum as she strode outside to collect her class for the afternoon session. She led the children into class and they seated themselves calmly as she took the register. The small, interlocking routines that they had developed together meant that in no time everyone was ready for the afternoon to begin.

'I've got an interesting question for us to look into this afternoon,' began Clover. 'I'd like us to explore some maths problems about time and distance.' The children looked up at her patiently. Miss Lightfoot reflected that at the start of the year there would have been semi-ritualised groans from the children at the very idea of tackling maths puzzles, but now they trusted Miss Lightfoot to make things fun or, at least, to make such activities interesting enough not to be a pain.

Clover only had the vaguest idea of what she wanted the children to learn but she did have a very clear sense of the particular range of problems that she wanted them to explore together. She only hoped that Mrs Chapman didn't pop her head around the door and ask her for a lesson plan.

After her first few years in teaching, Miss Lightfoot had given up making anything but the sketchiest plans for her lessons. Teaching a lesson was like public speaking, there was an optimal amount of planning to be done. Sometimes you needed more planning than other times and it was good to know what you were focussing on, but it was definitely unhelpful to pin down each exact thing that you were trying to say. Such an approach lacked flexibility and if the slightest thing happened to throw you off your meticulously planned course, you could easily find yourself all at sea.

From experience, Clover had discovered that the optimum level of preparation for her was simply the sense of a clear problem to solve. As she sat in front of her class at that moment, she found that she was wholly consumed by a problem that required a solution.

'I'm going to ask you all to run all the way home, right now,' said Clover. It was a daring opening gambit and the class watched her closely, several of them sporting rueful grins, wondering what her game really was. 'Let's imagine that you've got an important errand to run that means you have to get home as soon as you can,' she continued. It might be feeding your cat or realising that you've left a chocolate ice cream melting on the sofa. Whatever it is, I'd like you to work out how long it takes you to run home and then run all the way back to the school again. So how are you going to work out something like that?'

Hands were raised, 'We need to work out how fast we can run,' said Karl, who was one of Josh's group of friends.

'We also need to work out how long you can keep running for,' said a girl called Audrey. Clover wrote these up onto the board. All the time she was thinking herself about how long it would take someone to run all the way to Balfour Avenue where Dr Winter had lived and then make their way back to the school again. She was thinking of Mr Fish, Mrs Clegg and even, with some regret, Tom Flint. For any of those people to be the murderer they would have had to find their way to Dr Winter's house in the short window of time between the argument at the interval and the start of the parents' meeting.

'We need to work out exactly how far everyone would need to go to get home,' said Olivia. 'My house is quite a long way away and I usually come by car,' she added helpfully. 'So I think we're going to need the local studies maps.'

'I happen to have them right here,' said Miss Lightfoot, producing a tray of laminated maps from beneath one of the floral fabric drapes that covered her cupboards. 'Let's take the first ten minutes to talk together in your table-groups about how to solve this problem,' She looked up at the clock. 'At ten to two, I'll ask each group to tell us a little about their plans for investigating the problem and then we'll see if we can try some of them out,' she smiled at the children. 'Of course I'll be making my own plans to investigate too so we'll see what happens when we put our heads together.'

The first ten minutes of the lesson passed quickly and as the children presented their ideas to each other about how to investigate the time it would take to visit various local streets, Clover joined in with their thinking. As some of the children spread outside the room into part of the playground to investigate examples of running and distance, Clover herself started to think more about timing.

The range of estimates about the time it would take to run to and from Balfour Avenue went from three minutes to six minutes and Clover was inclined to agree with them. The children were working out distances to many different streets and they all fitted in with Clover's own guesses nicely. It would certainly have been possible for either Mr Fish, Mrs Clegg or Mr Flint to make it to Dr Winter's house and back with ease in the time they were unaccounted for.

Clover mused briefly about what the murderer had done when they'd arrived at his house. How quickly could someone discover that Dr Winter's report was so negative that it was worth killing him over it? Did they argue with Dr Winter about his findings? Was there time for that? Or perhaps they had already planned what they were going to do. Then there was the matter of typing out the false report and faxing it to the school after Dr Winter's death. Unfortunately thinking about this activity didn't rule out any of the three people she had in mind. Clover happened to know that both Mr Fish and Mrs Clegg were excellent typists, a necessity for their roles as senior managers and Tom was just as swift; she'd seen him at the computer many times, fingers flying over the keys as he typed things up for printing.

Despite having thought it all through, she found little comfort in the answers she'd arrived at. Mr Fish was still the most likely suspect because of his distressed condition and because he was the reason that the other two teachers were roaming around in the dark. However, despite the evidence, Clover couldn't imagine Simon taking enough initiative to follow through with such a terrible deed.

She glanced around the room. The notes that the children had made were either too sparse or so arcane that they were unintelligible. She hadn't specified how they were to investigate the problems they had been working on, though from the way she'd questioned the groups she knew they'd all been very well engaged on the tasks at hand. The children were chattering about the trivia they'd worked out about their relative journeys and how quickly a cheetah or a sloth would take to travel the distances they'd estimated. It was probably the best lesson she'd given in a couple of weeks, but if you only looked at what the children had produced in their books it appeared to be a disaster. She had bigger problems than getting the children to produce neat rows of sums for Mrs Chapman, she reflected, as she guided the children through packing up for the day and prepared herself for the staff meeting.

She hadn't cared for the way that Detective Meadows had been so quick to judge Mrs Chapman and now she had the feeling that the same thing was about to happen all over again with Simon Fish. This time, despite any doubts that Clover had, she didn't think anything could stop the big bad wolf from seizing upon his dinner.

14

The afternoon had passed quickly for Clover as she investigated how long it would take for someone to run to Balfour Avenue and back. However, her investigation only highlighted what she'd already guessed. It was certainly a possibility that someone at the school had slipped away and committed the crime, though she didn't think that Mr Fish had it in him. Still turning the puzzle over in her mind, Clover made her way to the staffroom for the emergency staff meeting. She had no idea what to expect.

The atmosphere in the staffroom was tense, to say the least. Janet Clegg was whispering almost conspiratorially with Mrs Chapman, to the surprise of Clover, since the two of them had been at each other's throats just a couple of hours earlier. Detective Meadows stood on his own, idly examining the notices scribbled on the staffroom blackboard. The rest of the staff were talking in hushed whispers as they made themselves tea before the meeting began. Clover approached Meadows boldly, 'Has anyone offered you a cup of tea?' she asked.

'They have, thank you Miss Lightfoot but I'm fine,' said Meadows, grimly.

'I take it you have bad news for us this evening?' Clover asked.

'I have news, certainly,' said Meadows. 'I'll let you be the judge of whether it's good or bad news for you all but it looks as if it will draw matters to a conclusion, at any rate.

'I shall be listening with interest,' said Clover. She was about to turn away when Meadows spoke again.

'You were most helpful this morning, Miss Lightfoot. Naturally, everything would have come out in the end but it's down to you that we were able to rule Mrs Chapman out of our enquiries as quickly as we did.' He smiled, 'My sister is a teacher. After seeing what she manages every day I've made it my business never to underestimate anyone who can succeed in your profession.'

'Thank you,' said Clover sincerely, though she was slightly uncomfortable with the finality of his tone. If everything was wrapped up already then that sounded like bad news for Mr Fish.

She found a seat and Janet Clegg took the lead. 'Welcome everyone and thank you for coming to this additional staff meeting. I have a great deal of information for you all that you'll need to absorb before you see the parents tomorrow morning.' Clover noted how Janet had framed her introduction to proceedings as if she were fully in command once more. Far from fighting her over this, Mrs Chapman looked rather smug. 'There are several items on today's agenda,' said Janet, 'firstly an important briefing from our visitor, Detective Meadows.' Meadows continued to stand while almost everyone else sat. A notable exception to this, Clover noticed, was Tom Flint, who stood next to the tea urn with his arms folded defensively. 'Following that,' said Janet, 'Mrs Chapman and I have some important news for you about the inspection of the school and the inspectorate organisations in general. But first, we will hear from Detective Meadows.'

Meadows eyed the staff before beginning to speak, as if checking for anything he might have missed, 'Some of you are aware that Dr Arthur Winter, Chief Inspector of Her Majesty's Inspectors of Schools lost his life last night under suspicious circumstances, at his home close to the school.' Meadows paused as there were gasps of shock from some around the room. 'We believe that Dr Winter left the school just after 7.35pm following a disagreement about the outcome of the recently completed school inspections. Distressed by the discussion, Dr Winter proceeded home, not realising that he was being followed by someone who was shortly to take his life.' Meadows ploughed on, 'We believe that the killer was known to Dr Winter because there was no sign of a forced entry to his house. Dr Winter welcomed someone into his home and, shortly afterwards, he died from a blow to the head delivered by a blunt object.'

Clover pressed her lips together and met Meadows' eyes as he continued. 'Most unusually, the killer did not flee the scene immediately but instead proceeded to type out a report that portrayed the school in a positive light, borrowing from Dr Winter's own words to make their case. They knew the telephone number for the office fax machine and they sent the falsified favourable report to the school before making their escape.' Meadows scowled. 'Dr Winter's body was discovered by Mrs Chapman, who chose to pay Dr Winter a visit when she heard that his report contained personal insults directed at her. She was at the scene when the constabulary arrived to investigate a call from a neighbour who had reported a disturbance.'

Now it was Meadows' turn to bite his lip. Clover watched him closely and saw that he wasn't comfortable about what he was going to say. 'We currently have someone who is working very closely with us to help with our enquiries. At this point in time I must inform you that the person in question is Mr Simon Fish, headmaster of this school.'

A hiss of whispers rose up around the room, most of them expressing disbelief and surprise. Clover found herself speaking up without being invited to contribute. 'Could I ask, Detective Meadows, do you have any direct evidence that Mr Fish committed this terrible crime? By *evidence* I mean something beyond the purely circumstantial lack of an alibi.' Janet Clegg and Mrs Chapman both looked daggers at Clover but Meadows answered her immediately.

'I'm afraid we do, Miss Lightfoot,' he said. 'Our enquiries have uncovered a witness who was walking his dog and recognised Dr Winter walking home, somewhat the worse for wear, accompanied by a man who precisely matches the description of Mr Simon Fish.' Meadows didn't look pleased about this but he seemed completely sure of his information. 'It seems that Mr Fish followed Dr Winters out of the school, perhaps to try to persuade him to write a more lenient report. He saw that Dr Winter had become intoxicated and helped him home. Soon afterwards, he may have discovered that Dr Winter wasn't about to change his negative report and the two of them may have disagreed, possibly violently. This may have resulted in the loss of Dr Winter's life. At this point it's possible that Mr Fish may have tried to falsify the school's inspection report before fleeing the scene. Because of the sensitive nature of this situation we're therefore continuing our enquires with the help of Mr Fish.'

'He's admitted it, you know,' chipped in Mrs Chapman, keeping a straight face but barely able to keep the glee out of her voice.

Meadows whirled around to fix her with a glare. 'In point of fact,' he said authoritatively, 'when confronted with the witness statement, Mr Fish admitted that he had indeed followed Dr Winter home with the intention of influencing the outcome of the inspection. This was information that he did not mention during his initial interview. However, he has continued to deny that he harmed Dr Winter, even though a witness has placed him at the scene of the crime with both the motive and the opportunity to commit the act in question. I cannot stress enough, however, that Mr Fish is innocent until proven guilty. We have merely reached the stage in our investigation when we have enough evidence to question him further.'

'Do *you* believe he's guilty?' asked Clover, surprising herself as she heard her own voice demanding a reply.

'At this time the evidence suggests that we are correct to name Mr Fish as someone who will need to help us with our enquiries, Miss Lightfoot but beyond that, the matter is out of my hands,' replied Meadows.

Before any more could be said, Janet Clegg took over again. 'The Chair of Governors, Mrs Sandy Delaney, has been hugely supportive in officially suspending Mr Fish from his duties while he is under suspicion and has appointed me as acting headteacher of the school until further notice. I have drafted a letter that will be sent to the parents tomorrow. However, we will also host a meeting for any concerned parents tomorrow morning because we believe that the news is likely to be reported by the national press.'

Mrs Clegg made a calming gesture with her hands as the staff began discussing the implications of her statement with each other. Clover saw Ellie looking suspiciously from Janet Clegg to Tom Flint, who didn't seem surprised by the news at all. Janet spoke up again over the noise and requested their attention for a moment longer. 'As far as the school inspection reports are concerned, they will soon receive national attention. Mrs Chapman has been very helpful in offering her advice about how best to proceed.' Mrs Clegg waved Mrs Chapman forward to speak and she stepped up, exuding an air of righteous indignation.

'This school's abysmal standards under the leadership of Mr Fish have been highlighted by the tragic events of the last twenty-four hours. My first response was to consider continuing the Ofsted inspection process beyond its current remit in order to make our case for all of the improvements that needed to be made.' Mrs Chapman offered the room an icy smile, 'However, after extended discussions with Mrs Clegg, the new *acting* headteacher, we have come to an agreement. This school will be the first to enter what we at Ofsted are calling "very special measures." At this point, the suspension of Mr Fish while he *helps the police with their enquiries* will at least provide the school with a fresh start, albeit with the understanding that this institution is, without doubt, the worst example of bad practice in the entire country at this time. This is a situation we shall help Mrs Clegg rectify as we support her in leading a rigorous campaign of school improvement that will require the support of everyone in the school community.'

Mrs Chapman smiled, 'On a broader level, I don't mind confiding in you that the powers that be are absolutely horrified by the mess that's been permitted to arise by Dr Winter's HMIs and they have moved swiftly to put the entire resources of both inspection organisations under my personal control.' Mrs Chapman was almost glowing with satisfaction at these words.

'What about Antonia Reynolds?' asked Clover bluntly. 'I had heard she was in line to take over from Dr Winter's role as Chief Inspector of the HMIs?'

'That is no longer the case,' said Mrs Chapman. 'I intend to offer Antonia the opportunity to apply for a lesser role at Ofsted but there really isn't any reason for her job in its current form to exist, as it would simply duplicate my own.' Clover looked from Mrs Chapman to Mrs Clegg. It looked like they had sewn it all up very nicely between the two of them in the course of the afternoon. Mrs Clegg had been shockingly quick to take over the school and Mrs Chapman had used the opportunity to swallow all that remained of Dr Winter's organisation into her own. At the same time they had condemned the school to *very special measures*, whatever that meant. It seemed to mean that they had agreed to say that all the teachers were terrible at their jobs. Clover had a thousand things she wanted to say but any one of them was too difficult or too unspeakable to voice out loud. It looked to Clover as if Janet had thrown Simon under the bus and the school's reputation with him in order to gain a promotion herself.

'This will certainly be in the newspapers by tomorrow morning,' said Janet Clegg briskly, 'so we have called an emergency meeting of the board of governors later tonight to be sure that they are all properly aware of the situation beforehand. I advise you all to go home and get a good night's sleep and we'll face the music together tomorrow. Unless there are any further questions, I suggest we end the meeting here.' The meeting didn't need any more encouragement than that to break up.

Ellie rushed to Clover's side. 'It's all so awful,' she said helplessly. 'When you hear it spelled out so plainly like that it sounds completely brutal.'

'It does, doesn't it?' said Clover who was watching Janet and Mrs Chapman shake hands on the other side of the busy room. 'I still can't believe it,' Clover said. 'I spoke to Simon just this morning and he seemed completely innocent to me, I still don't believe he was lying to me, I wouldn't have thought he was that good a liar...I wouldn't have thought he was that good at anything, to be honest.'

'He was lying to everyone,' said Ellie, 'even the police, it seems. At least you don't have to suspect Tom of anything any more,' she said. 'That's important to you, isn't it?'

'What?' said Clover suddenly blushing.

'You heard me,' said Ellie with a wicked giggle. 'Now that we know Mr Fish was with Dr Winter and lying about it, then we can be pretty sure it wasn't anything to do with Tom or Janet.'

'Can we?' said Clover thoughtfully, 'It looks like Janet has gained more than anyone out of all this trouble and Tom looks like someone who's done something he regrets.'

Clover looked across at Tom Flint who was still standing by the tea urn in the corner. He didn't look like someone who was worried about his job or even someone who was horrified by the revelations about Mr Fish. He looked like someone who was feeling very uncomfortable and possibly rather guilty about something. Whatever was going on there, Clover decided to put her feelings to one side until she'd got to the bottom of it.

'Clover Lightfoot,' said Ellie brightly, 'or should I say *Detective* Lightfoot, I think the stress of all this has been too much for you. Goodness knows it would have affected me if I'd been trying to put on a school play while the inspectors were staging a Punch and Judy show before my eyes. You have had two very long days and you probably need to have a good rest. It sounds as if things are not going to get much easier in the next few days either, so why don't you just give that brain of yours a break?'

Ellie's cheery tone broke Clover's concentration and she gave her friend a smile. 'Alright,' she said, 'life has to go on, doesn't it? I just have a few things to take care of before I go home and I'll probably need a piece of cake just to keep me going.'

15

Clover took herself and her cake back to her classroom. Looking at the pile of children's books on her desk, full of the notes from the afternoon's work, she wondered whether there was any point in going through them all and ticking them. She certainly didn't have time to analyse all the things the children had come up with. They'd already given their feedback when they presented their ideas to the class so the notes in the books had already served their purpose. She went through them very quickly, glancing at the notes and diagrams the children had drawn to help them work out walking speed and distance over time.

There was something particular about Sequoia's that caught her eye. Her usually neat work had been scribbled over furiously and the page was a mess. Clover flicked back through Sequoia's rough book and noted that all the previous pages were filled with perfectly orderly notes and drawings. Puzzled, Clover wondered what was distressing her. As far as she knew, the children didn't even know about the murder of Dr Winter, let alone that Mr Fish was the chief suspect. Clover made a mental note to ask Sequoia what had provoked this reaction then she put the book on one side and quickly looked through the rest.

After rifling through the books for half hour or so, Clover fell into a malaise. She tidied up a few things around her desk but then realised that she'd been standing in the middle of her classroom, lost in contemplation, for ages. She could think of dozens of important things that she could usefully get on with but she didn't seem to be doing any of them. Instead, her thoughts kept returning to the suspiciously guilty look on Tom Flint's face in the staff meeting and she knew that she wouldn't manage to do anything else until she'd put her mind at rest.

Tom Flint taught the ten- and eleven-year-old children of the top juniors and Clover found him in his classroom with a box labelled 'Work Tray Three' set on the table in front of him, along with a large piece of grey sugar paper full of rough but purposeful diagrams.

'I didn't know you'd started working on the Egyptians with your class,' said Clover.

'Hi there,' said Tom cheerfully. 'No, we haven't, we're still doing the Romans and the Greeks.'

'It's just that your drawing looks a lot like hieroglyphics to me,' said Clover as she peered at the paper.

Tom looked down at his sketches and laughed, 'Perhaps modern hieroglyphics that only members of the tiny civilisation of Mr Flint's class could ever understand. These are teaching points from the writing that the children did today. If there's something I want to explain to everyone, I'll make a few notes of the examples as I go. If I draw them out, I can stick up this piece of paper and talk the whole class through them.'

'What's that?' asked Clover, pointing at something that looked like a stick man being chased by a snake.

'It's a diagram to remind me that some of the children are writing in the passive voice, so I'm going to make a teaching point out of spotting the difference. My example will be a sentence like,"The snake chases Tom." The snake is the subject of the sentence and it's actively doing the chasing.' Tom tapped his diagram as he explained. 'Then we'll see if they can spot a passive sentence when we talk about Tom being chased by the snake.'

'Poor Tom,' said Clover, 'so passive in both examples, whether he's the subject of the sentence or not.'

'Tom,' said Tom, 'is wise enough not to mess with a snake and doesn't mind being called passive if it means he doesn't get an ankle full of venom.' The two of them exchanged smiles. 'How can I help you, Clover?' he asked warmly.

'Oh just provide a distraction for a minute or two, will you?' said Clover. She suddenly felt much too sleepy to think very much about anything else. 'Tell me about something normal, my brain is too full of unusual and horrible thoughts.'

'I do have something distracting that you might like,' said Tom with a grin. He turned around the pile of books he was working his way through and showed them to Clover. 'I've had my class writing reviews of your childrens' play. They all loved having you as their teacher last year and it was a real treat for them to watch your class rehearse their scenes. We did the reviews as a writing exercise in its own right but I also thought it might be nice for your class to get some proper, positive comments about their show.'

Clover found she was glowing slightly, warmed by his gesture. She picked up the first of the books and looked at the name on the front. 'How is Charlie getting on this year? I do miss him, when I have time to miss anyone, that is.'

Tom smiled, 'He's a delight. He credits you with teaching him what adverbs are.'

Clover sniggered, 'Please thank him kindly, gratefully and wholeheartedly for me, won't you?'

'I'll pass that on,' said Tom and then fell silent as he watched Clover rifle through the child's book to look at what her old pupil had written. Clover beamed as she read the review and glanced at Tom shyly.

'That's lovely,' she said. Then, reading from the child's book, 'Josh and Jake's version of *Julius Caesar* made it very clear that it really didn't matter if Caesar wanted to take over Rome or not; his friends killed him because they were afraid of his power.'

'That's good writing,' said Tom. 'I'm sure it comes from all the work you did with them last year, they've all picked up a little of your style from working with you.'

'Mr Flint, you flatter me,' said Clover happily.

'Some of the children have developed some interesting views on Shakespeare,' said Tom. 'Tavleen now thinks that the best part of King Lear is when the mermaid destroys the King of Spain's fleet.'

'Oh dear! If she ever goes to see it performed properly she's in for a disappointing night out.'

'I think Noah really got it,' said Tom. 'He says your Richard III was brilliantly "hunchbacky." He's quick to praise whoever was playing the part of the hunch for managing to hang on when King Richard jumped on the back of the donkey.'

'Yes, that was Alfie,' said Clover, 'I tried to persuade him that King Richard's hunched back wasn't a speaking part, but he overruled me citing artistic reasons.'

'It certainly it brought a whole new perspective to the piece,' said Tom. 'Asher wrote about how your production of *Romeo and Juliet* showed that the unlucky couple was ultimately separated by a lack of modern conveniences and basic organisational skills.'

'That does say something about the nature of tragedy doesn't it?' said Clover, thoroughly enjoying herself.

'You know, I studied that exact question at Uni,' said Tom. 'Academically speaking, I think the point Shakespeare is making in Romeo and Juliet is about the difference between passion and bravery. They're certainly very passionately motivated to be together but they don't have the conviction to follow through with what they want to do and they can only scheme at it, so it all ends in disaster.'

'That certainly is a tragedy,' said Clover catching Tom's eye.

'Or it's about people being completely irrational about what they want and refusing to be reasonable in any way,' said Tom.

'Tom, are you still talking about Romeo and Juliet?' Clover fixed him with a meaningful look.

'No, you've got me,' said Tom, 'I can't help thinking about the murder. It's so horrible. I try to shut it out but then it sneaks back into my thoughts. I can't imagine Mr Fish doing anything like this but he must have been completely desperate about the inspection reports. I keep telling myself that I really did do absolutely everything that could be done but I can't be sure.'

Clover caught a sense of the same discomfort she'd seen in him earlier and probed to find out what he might mean. 'What do you mean when you said you'd done absolutely everything you could?'

Tom shifted uneasily in his seat, 'I just meant that we all went to enormous lengths to see if we could make things work out well and despite all of that it didn't make any difference.'

Having followed the scent this far, Clover asked him directly. 'Tom, what enormous lengths did you go to?'

Tom looked intensely uncomfortable for a moment and Clover almost took her question back. She only hesitated when she thought of Simon Fish and the fact that he was probably looking at the inside of a jail cell at that very moment. So she hung on, waiting patiently, and eventually Tom answered her, 'Well, Sandy Delaney came to see me a couple of weeks ago, just after the inspections were announced. She said a friend was visiting from out of town.' Tom paused for a moment and went to close his classroom door. He sat back down again but he couldn't meet Clover's eyes as he continued his story.

'Go on,' said Clover.'

Tom nodded without looking up at her, 'Well, Sandy Delaney said that her friend was a lovely woman but was still looking for the right person.' He shrugged, 'I don't know if you know this about me but I'm single at the moment and it's quite hard to meet someone when you work in teaching.'

'Yes,' said Clover, wide-eyed with incredulity, 'it is, isn't it?' Tom kept on gazing at his own shoes and Clover wondered where all this was leading.

'I took up Sandy on her offer and she arranged a blind date with her friend,' said Tom. 'I never imagined that her friend would be Amanda Chapman.'

'What?' said Clover, snapping out of her own interest in Tom instantly. 'Mrs Chapman, the inspector? Isn't she married?' Clover asked.

'Not any more: apparently she's separated but she's keeping her married name because she thinks it will help her career.'

'How so?'

'Well, I think her former husband has some friends in high places,' Tom couldn't bring himself to look up at Clover.

'I see,' said Clover. 'The evening didn't go well?'

'No,' said Tom, 'I'm not very good in intimate situations,' he shook his head, 'I'm fine when I'm teaching or even when I'm with someone who knows what I'm like,' he nodded in Clover's direction, 'but I can get terribly awkward otherwise.'

'What happened?' asked Clover.

'Well, I guess I was nervous and I ended up talking about my family a little too much. In the end Amanda had to actually tell me that I was supposed to be paying her more attention and not be so self-centred.'

'Sounds like Mrs Chapman is just as charming personally as she is professionally,' said Clover, 'talking about your family isn't a bad thing you know, Tom? I think a lot of women would find it quite charming to hear more about you.'

'I did mention my sister at least twice, so I can see how she thought I must have been going on about them.'

'That's still not unreasonable, if you ask me.'

Tom shrugged, 'it probably came up because we got off to such a bad start. I really didn't know you're supposed to bring a gift to a thing like that.'

'A gift?' said Clover, her brows climbing to new heights, 'I wouldn't have thought you'd do that either, what did she give you?'

'Oh nothing, it doesn't work that way around apparently. You know, it's sort of the done thing that the man is supposed to do, like paying for dinner and the taxi and stuff.'

'You got a taxi together? To her place?' Clover swallowed, feeling somewhat anxious about what she might hear next.

'No, no, it was pretty clear we weren't getting along so I paid for a taxi to take her home from the restaurant. I think it was pretty obvious that there wasn't going to be a second date. To be honest she made me a little uncomfortable. She was so aggressive, you know?'

'Aggressive? What did she do, try to kiss you?' asked Clover, barely able to hide her horror at the thought.

'Oh no, nothing like that,' said Tom. 'She kind of assaulted one of the waitresses though, when the lady came to clear up our plates.'

'No! Why?'

'She gave her a little lecture on serving food from one side and taking away the empty dishes from the other side and then sort of slapped her.'

Clover's jaw had dropped, 'Mrs Chapman actually slapped a waitress for picking up her plate from the wrong side of the table?'

'Yeah, I mean she only tapped the waitress on her hand but it seemed like she was trying to slap her harder and it was pretty awkward. I definitely didn't want to see her again after that. So it really made things more difficult when she started coming to observe my lessons.'

'Tom, that sounds horrible and a real conflict of interests for you. I'm not surprised you felt uncomfortable: I think anyone would have felt really strange after that. Is that why you seemed so uncomfortable in the staffroom today?'

'Probably. It was just seeing Amanda....Mrs Chapman again. I thought we'd seen the last of each other after she gave me feedback from my last lesson. I'd really tried my hardest and I thought things went well but she's got a lot more experience than me so I have to accept her judgement.'

Clover shook her head. It all sounded very wrong, 'I don't think you have to accept anything unquestioningly. If she's being so critical of you then she has to at least tell you her opinion of how you can improve. Did she say anything about that?'

'She just said I really had to make much more of an effort. She said that quite a few times but we had to stop the interview because she had something in her eye that was bothering her.'

'What?'

'Yeah, it was really strange actually, she said she couldn't stop her eye from twitching and it was embarrassing because it must have looked like she was winking at me. She apologised for it and she said she hoped it didn't distract me from what she was trying to communicate. I told her I got the message and that I'd try to improve my lessons. That was really all I could do.'

Clover shuddered and shook her head, it sounded like Mrs Chapman had been literally winking at him but thankfully for Tom, he hadn't understood. 'Tom, it sounds to me like you were being harassed,' Clover said.

Tom laughed, 'Me? I don't think it works like that, does it?'

Clover shook her head firmly. 'Imagine if the genders were reversed, it would certainly be harassment then, wouldn't it? It works both ways, you know! There's a reason you're feeling uncomfortable about all of this. It sounds to me like she was trying to bribe you with a better rating for your lesson if you offered her a second date.'

Tom looked puzzled, 'But why would she want a second date when the first one was so terrible anyway?'

'Well it sounds to me like she didn't really mind being taken out for an all-expenses-paid evening where she constantly talked about herself and explained how you and the waitress could jump through more hoops to please her.'

'It wasn't like that...I don't think,' said Tom uncertainty, finally finding the courage to meet Clover's eyes again.

Clover was angry on his behalf, 'I think it was exactly like that. Sandy Delaney has a lot to answer for,' said Clover. 'She obviously wanted the school to get a good report.' Clover shook her head. 'I can't believe Sandy would have stooped to setting you up with Mrs Chapman just to improve our chances! On the other hand, perhaps Sandy Delaney is capable of doing anything that suited her purposes, regardless of whom she hurts along the way.'

'You don't think she could have had anything to do with the murder, do you?' asked Tom.

'I don't know,' said Clover. 'Sandy's not someone I've ever considered as a suspect before.'

'But if Mr Fish was behind the murder of Dr Winter, then Sandy can't have done it.'

'I'm not necessarily suggesting she did anything herself,' said Clover, 'but she might have pulled some strings to make it happen, just as she pulled your strings and Mrs Chapman's too. Whether she did or didn't have anything to do with the murder, I'm going to have a word with her about this.'

'What?' asked Tom, his voice edged with panic. 'I don't want any trouble.'

'Oh believe me, there won't be any trouble,' said Clover coldly, 'I won't bring up the games she's been playing with you, I promise, but I intend to get to the bottom of all this, one way or another.'

16

Clover left Tom to his marking and headed directly for the staffroom. She was aware of the sound of her heels clacking angrily on the wooden floor as she marched down the corridor. It was a very good bet that Sandy Delaney was in the staffroom by now, getting herself a cup of tea before the governors' meeting and Clover meant to have a conversation with her.

Clover glanced at her watch. She had observed a meeting only once before. It wasn't private, so anyone from the staff could sit in on the governors' meetings if they wished, but this open-door policy usually meant very little. This was because the meetings were so exhaustingly boring. For her part, Clover was just thankful she didn't have to discuss the school's response to updated fire regulations or new formats for reporting the way in which the school's budget was spent.

A slip of paper with the words MEETING IN PROGRESS was stuck to the staffroom door with a single, off-centre blob of Blu-tac, but the door stood ajar and Clover saw that people were still milling about, getting themselves cups of tea and slices of what remained of the cakes. Clover slipped into the room and immediately saw that Sandy Delaney was in close conversation with Janet Clegg and Mrs Chapman. The three of them looked as if they were having an extremely friendly conversation and Clover felt her blood run cold, having a sudden vision of the three witches from Macbeth. She had a nasty feeling that almost everything that could be said to calm things down was already too little, too late. There were friendlier faces in the staffroom too, at least. Bettina Williams was setting out some boxes of juice and drinking glasses and she gave Clover a carefree wave as Janet called the room to order.

Halted in her pursuit of Sandy, Clover took a seat in one of the comfy staffroom chairs. She looked around: she wasn't the only one who had come to watch. A couple of the teaching assistants, who were also parents of children at the school, had come along too, perhaps having caught a whiff of the forthcoming scandal. There certainly wouldn't be any keeping of secrets from the parents after the meeting tonight. Phones would no doubt be ringing off the hook as the revelations spread through the local community.

The school governors sat together at the table in the centre of the room. Sandy Delaney looked very much in charge of proceedings but it was Janet Clegg, sitting next to her, who spoke up first. 'I call this meeting of the board of school governors to order and, for the benefit of our guests, I move that all attendees briefly introduce themselves.'

'Seconded,' chirruped Sandy Delaney as she beamed around the room at everyone. 'I'm Sandy Delaney and I've been Chair of the board of governors for several years now. I'm a parent governor and my lovely daughter, Olivia, is in year 5.' She nodded benevolently in Clover's direction, not appearing to notice that the cheerful Miss Lightfoot was not looking very pleased with anyone at that moment in time.

Seated on the other side of Sandy was Mrs Clydesdale, the school secretary, who, it seemed, had a starring role on these occasions. 'Mrs Delilah Clydesdale,' announced Mrs Clydesdale, 'Secretary to the school and this meeting. I shall be recording the minutes and decisions of the board.' '*Delilah!*' Despite her anger, Clover felt her eyebrows pop up at hearing Mrs Clydesdale's full name: she never would have guessed that the fearsome guardian of the front office was secretly a *Delilah*.

'Mrs Amanda Chapman,' said Mrs Chapman who was next to speak, 'Head of Ofsted and acting Chief Inspector of Her

Majesty's Inspectorate.' Clover looked at her suspiciously but everyone else was already looking at the first of the two men seated at the end of the table.

'Reverend Clifford Smalling,' said a white-haired, bespectacled man. He was very casually dressed and he tried to include everyone as he nodded around the room. 'I'm the vicar at All Saints and everyone's welcome to pop in any time...of course,' he added confidentially, 'we usually only see most of you at Christmas but at times like these...' he trailed off again with a gesture of helplessness. 'Oh, and call me Cliff,' he added as an afterthought, dragging everyone's attention back to him once more.

'Nigel Champion,' declared the balding gentleman who sat at the end of the table. 'Local businessman, retired,' he said, flexing his shoulders in his blazer and straightening his blue and burgundy tie. Clover remembered Nigel from her previous visit to this meeting and she took a deep breath, steeling herself to listen to the kinds of things he might say this time. The last time she'd attended he'd given a fifteen minute lecture on the value of including Latin in the primary school curriculum. It had taken most of the meeting to explain to him that decisions about the curriculum weren't part of the governors' remit. He'd actually accepted this quite quickly when it was preceded by the words, '*point of order*;' procedural language of this kind had an almost magical effect on him. Nigel was seated at the end of the table and he gestured to the final member of the board who had only just taken her seat opposite him.

It was Bettina Williams. 'I think everyone knows me by now,' she said. 'I'm Jake and Josh's mum and I see you all often enough for one reason or another.' She looked across to Janet Clegg to complete the introductions.

'Mrs Janet Clegg, acting headteacher,' said Janet unable to resist shaking her head slightly as she spoke the words. Clover stifled a sigh that threatened to become too much of an open expression of exasperation as the meeting began.

Janet continued to lead, 'Everyone here is now aware that Mr Simon Fish has agreed to help the police with their enquiries about the suspicious death of Dr Winter. Naturally, we're keen to ensure that the children don't suffer any inconvenience as a result of Mr Fish's *actions*. To this end, I have been working with Sandy and our colleague from Ofsted, Mrs Chapman, on a statement that announces the suspension of Mr Fish and my appointment as acting headteacher. We'd like to agree that statement with you this evening before we release it to the parents and the press.'

'Excuse me,' said Clover. 'Is it really fair to release this statement without even informing Mr Fish or giving him the chance to defend himself?'

Sandy hesitated for a moment but Mrs Chapman leapt in swiftly. 'Is it fair to the children to expose them to a headteacher who is suspected of murder?'

'Has he been charged with anything?' asked Clover.

'I would suggest that the police procedure that is taking place now isn't the most important point,' said Mrs Chapman.

'In point of fact,' said Nigel Champion authoritatively, 'being charged with a crime is a very different matter to being suspected of a crime and questioned by the authorities.'

'What an interesting observation,' said Clover, trying to goad Nigel into saying more, if he set his mind to it he could slow things down quite a bit.

'Dear Mr Fish did always seem to be such a nice man,' said Reverend Smalling. 'I do recall you yourself describing his gentle nature as his saving grace,' he added, addressing Janet Clegg, who looked openly irritated at the direction in which the conversation was progressing.

Clover had introduced just enough doubt into the minds of the board to slow proceedings down and make them think about what they were doing, but Sandy wasn't about to let Clover get away with it. She weighed her words carefully. 'As Chair of Governors, I must say I don't think we can really permit Mr Fish to occupy a position of responsibility while the police are undertaking the *due process of the law*,' she said, aiming her words directly at Nigel.

'Quite right, quite right,' said Nigel almost interrupting her with his enthusiasm to agree, 'mustn't interfere with the *due process of the law*, that's paramount, of course.'

Clover was already preparing to steer him back into delaying the agreement again when she saw Bettina Williams waving to her silently from the other end of the table. Clover's words caught on her lips and she turned to her friend in confusion.

'Sorry! Sorry everyone!' said Bettina in a stage whisper. 'It's just that I realised I absolutely must have a word with Miss Lightfoot about my boys Jake and Josh and now's my only opportunity.'

'Isn't this somewhat untimely, Mrs Williams?' asked Nigel. Bettina only shrugged with a helpless smile. 'I suppose so, but needs must. If you have to carry on without me, please do.' Bettina led a confused Clover out of the staffroom and closed the door behind them.

'Bettina,' asked Clover in a hushed voice, 'what's the matter with the boys?'

Without missing a beat Bettina answered, '...their headmaster is about to be revealed as a horrible criminal and I don't want it ruining their chances of getting into a decent secondary school. That's what's the matter!'

Et tu Bettina, thought Clover.

'But Bettina, surely you can't be happy with rushing this through and destroying Mr Fish's reputation just because he's a suspect in a case? Anyone might be suspected of anything but it's not grounds for being thrown out of your job.'

'I understand that, said Bettina, but I intend to send my boys to a really lovely, private secondary school in two years' time and there's going to be a lot of competition for places. If my boys are only known as the ones who came from the school with the murderous headmaster then they're not going to be the ones who get in.'

'Bettina,' said Clover, pleadingly, 'this is terribly wrong. They're all trying to push this through because they think it's the best way to protect the school but it means they're treating Mr Fish as if he had already been found guilty. I just don't think we should jump to conclusions.'

Bettina looked at Clover seriously. 'Since when have you been such a big fan of Mr Fish? How many times have we rolled our eyes at something he's done, or more importantly, something he's failed to do.'

'My opinions on Mr Fish's abilities as a headteacher have got nothing to do with whether he's a criminal or not,' said

Clover, shocked that Bettina couldn't see the difference between disapproving of Mr Fish's work and seeing him being pronounced guilty by the press. 'Sandy, Janet and Mrs Chapman are jumping the gun on this and it's wrong. You don't know what they're capable of.'

Bettina shook her head, 'If you're talking about Sandy setting up Tom Flint with Mrs Chapman, well, everyone's known about that for ages.'

'What? I didn't know until just now,' said Clover indignantly.

'Well, you're the only one that didn't because Sandy told everyone what she was up to. We all thought it was a bit of a hoot and it might even have worked if they'd hit it off, don't you think?'

'I can't believe you approve of this. Tom ended up feeling very uncomfortable about it.'

'Oh, he's a big boy,' said Bettina. 'He'll get over it and from what I hear there's no need to be jealous, everyone knows he's got a *thing* for you.'

Clover was horrified to find herself being gossiped about so openly.

'Look, Clover, *darling,*' said Bettina. 'You're practically the perfect teacher and you wouldn't believe the favours me and Sandy called in to get our children into your class. But that's just the way things work. It's right and proper that you have a fantastic sense of fair play, but are you really going to put your own reputation on the line for someone as pathetic as Mr Fish? Stop trying to make all of this better. Go home, have a good rest and concentrate on looking after the children tomorrow. Leave the dirty work to the parents. We don't mind it at all, heaven knows I'll do whatever it takes to make sure my boys get the very best and I'm not about to start apologising for that, to you or to anyone else for that matter.'

Clover was stunned to hear all of this coming from Bettina, who'd always seemed such a good and selfless person. She rubbed her eyes and took a deep breath. 'Go home,' said Bettina, gently. 'It's probably going to be horrible tomorrow and the children are going to need you.' Clover couldn't meet

Bettina's eye as she pulled away from her former friend and walked back to her classroom.

The school building was quiet now with only the distant sounds of the cleaners finishing up the last of their work. Clover felt tired and much older than her years. She was suddenly imagining the conversations the parents had been having about her and it made the classroom suddenly seem small and sad, as if the bubble of happiness and kindness that she'd tried to create for the children had been popped.

A scratching noise in the near-silence caught her attention and she realised that the sleepy honey-coloured rabbit that belonged to the class had woken up. 'Hello Pudding,' she said, 'you understand don't you?' The rabbit blinked at her rapidly and twitched its little nose. Clover managed a tiny smile.

Clover turned back towards her desk and noticed that half a bar of luxury chocolate had been left there waiting for her. Ellie must have put it there for her as she'd left school for the day. Her friend's thoughtfulness was too much and for a moment Clover felt herself start to cry. Blinking away the tears she managed a tiny laugh and snapped off a couple of pieces of the dark, brittle chocolate. The taste was exquisite and it seemed all the more intense in quiet of the darkened room. Still savouring the chocolate, she went to the rabbit hutch and gently lifted Pudding up into her arms. The bunny looked up at her wisely before tucking his head down into the crook of her arm. Clover plucked a leaf of basil from one of the pots of herbs that the class were growing and tempted Pudding with a taste. Pudding shuddered with the intense flavour and started to struggle to get another nibble. She placed the leaf in Pudding's pen and gently put him down, stroking his ears as she did so.

However difficult it might seem just then, Clover thought, in the morning the children would arrive, ready to learn, she would have a chance to make a difference to their lives and whatever else was going on would seem very small in comparison to that. She took a deep breath, picked up her things and went home.

17

Clover never had a problem sleeping after spending all day with the children and, despite the games being played by the adults, that night was no exception. She slept soundly and met the new day with fresh resolve to concentrate on helping the children through an odd and confusing time. Arriving in the school, she stopped at the school office and checked her pigeonhole. Sure enough something was waiting for her there. It was a neatly typed letter that had been photocopied onto bright pink paper to make it stand out. A similarly fluorescent copy lay in each of the other pigeonholes, ready for the staff to collect as they came into work. Clover picked up her copy and skimmed through it. It felt very odd to be reading about Mr Fish's suspension as headteacher and the statement was very brief. Absently, she looked through the other items in case there was anything that she'd missed.

The longest-term occupant of her pigeonhole was a dusty, stapled copy of the staff handbook. The handbook was made up of typed notes reproduced in livid, purple dye created with an ancient banda machine. Despite the comprehensive nature of this archaic document, Clover was sure there was nothing in the handbook that would help her with the current crisis.

The only other loose item awaiting her attention was a three-week-old directive from Mr Fish about displaying children's paintings by mounting them on two different colours of backing paper. This was to be done consistently, the note said, in order to show how much the school placed a high value on the children's artistic expression. Clover looked at the note sadly. This missive had been produced in a flurry of activity during the short window between the announcement of the inspections and their commencement and it had never been mentioned by anyone since. Clover paused to throw it in the bin but found herself hesitating out of a sudden feeling of pity for Simon Fish.

As she set up her room for the day's activities, Clover re-read the statement for parents about Dr Winter's murder. This time, she thought about the implications of the statement being sent to all the parents. The statement was carefully phrased. It didn't accuse Simon of being guilty of anything, yet, but it certainly implied that it was only a matter of time before the police charged him. Maybe that wasn't even unfair, Clover reflected sadly. Despite her own observations of Mr Fish, it was still possible that he was the murderer after all.

Suddenly, something in the statement caught her eye and Clover let out a shocked laugh. She rushed out of the room and headed quickly for the headteacher's office. She rapped on the door firmly and a voice called out for her to enter. 'Hi Janet,' said Clover when she stepped inside, but she was immediately taken aback. She had expected to find Janet Clegg in Simon's office but she hadn't expected to see the office totally transformed. The desk had been turned around to face the door in a formal manner and it had been cleared of anything except essential office equipment. The display boards were clear of Mr Fish's bubble writing although anything made by the children had been left in place. One half of the office was heaped with overflowing boxes that had been previously covered up by Mr Fish's coloured drapes. Janet had taken control of the space in a matter of hours.

'Clover,' said Janet Clegg firmly but coolly, 'I was hoping to speak to you at some point today.'

'Oh, really?' asked Clover. She rather thought Janet might have avoided her after Clover's performance at the governors' meeting.

'Of course,' said Janet smoothly, 'I wanted to reassure you that you're a hugely respected member of the staff and I wanted to say that I'm sorry if this disruption has been particularly hard on you.'

'Thank you, Janet,' said Clover accepting the peace offering at face value.

Janet continued, 'I need to know that all the staff are behind me during this difficult time,' she said meaningfully.

'I appreciate that Janet,' said Clover, 'I still don't think what happened seems quite right but I just thought you should know that there's a typo on your statement.'

'What? Oh no, where?' exclaimed Janet, losing her composure completely. The slightly condescending tone left her voice and she leaned forward as Clover placed the statement on the table.

'Well,' said Clover, 'I don't think that you meant to describe Dr Winter as a great *fiend* to the school. The letter R is sticky on Simon's...' Clover corrected herself, 'On *that* typewriter, Mr Fish used to make mistakes because of it all the time.'

Janet flushed, horrified, then started to laugh. 'At least Mrs Clydesdale hasn't made copies for the parents yet, will you help me fix this?' she asked.

'Of course,' said Clover, 'that's why I'm here.'

Janet melted at once, 'Oh Clover, thank you. I can't tell you how much it means to have you on board. Can you get the bad copies from the pigeonholes while I correct the original?' Clover nodded and dashed off while Janet found her original copy and started to look for a bottle of correcting fluid. It was barely fifteen minutes before they'd covered up the mistake and Janet had typed out the correction over the top. The two of them exchanged relieved smiles and things almost seemed normal again by the time the bell was rung for the start of the day.

When Clover went out into the playground to greet the class as they lined up to go inside, she could see that the parents were troubled by the news that was going around and only about half the class were present. She might have expected that some of the parents would keep their children at home until they'd heard the full story about what had taken place but she didn't think this many would stay away.

She'd expected the parents might want to talk to her but in fact the opposite was the case. The parents that had brought their children to school had gathered around Bettina or Sandy in the further corners of the playground, no doubt making sure that they all sang from the same song sheet when it came to the terrible story of Mr Fish, the failed headteacher and possible murderer.

Only nine children followed Clover into the classroom this morning so rather than calling out everyone's names, she ticked those few names quickly and sent Holly to the office with the register. Clover asked the small group to come and fill up the tables nearest to her own desk and then began the day's work.

'Let's start with a question,' she said. 'What have you heard about what has happened at our school?'

'Mr Fish hurt someone,' said Jake with certainty.

'Alright,' said Clover. 'What else have people heard?'

'It was the Prime Minister,' said Chloe wisely, 'Mr Fish punched him until he died.'

Clover drew a breath and paused to decide which way she'd go about dismantling this idea. 'The Prime Minister?' she asked, curiously.

'He's an important person from the government,' said Chloe.

'Well, there are lots of people who work for the government,' said Clover, 'and a lot of them do important jobs, so you're right about some of those things but I happen to know that the Prime Minister is alive and well. Jake, you're right that people are asking Mr Fish some questions about what happened on the night of our school play and you're also right that someone who worked for the government got hurt, but nobody is sure what happened just yet. The police are working it all out very carefully, just like we would work out what happened if there was a fight in the playground.'

'Did someone really die?' asked Sequoia quietly.

'Yes,' said Clover, addressing this directly. 'Someone called Dr Winter who was helping the school and he was hurt by someone who visited his house. Sadly he died. Nothing bad happened here at the school and we don't think anyone's in the slightest danger or we'd have told you all to stay at home.' Holly started to cry and Clover caught her eye. 'What do we know about living and dying?' Hands crept up and Clover picked out children to take turns in answering. The children's ideas about death were as varied and patchy as their ideas about anything else. Ideas came rushing forth in a babble about the afterlife, better places and worse places that people went when they died and what happened to human bodies when they were buried. Clover would have found it hard to think about it too closely if she weren't responding to the children directly. After she'd drawn out everything that the children were thinking about she reprised the seven signs of life that they'd studied earlier that year and talked about what physically happens when life ends. The children were sombre but very calm, picking up on the mood that Clover was projecting as they talked about such a serious subject. When it came to the matter of what happened to people after they had died, Clover summarised that people had different beliefs about that.

She then set the children working on a short task about the seven signs of life but quickly noticed that Sequoia had retreated into the tiny covered area in the book corner. Clover took a quick tour of her class and prompted a couple of the children who were struggling to work as a pair before circling back to check on Sequoia. Sequoia had her book on her lap and she had already written out quick definitions of respiration and movement. She looked up as Clover sat down on the cushions beside her, just outside the secluded area of the book nook.

'Sequoia, do you know anything else about what happened on the night of the play?' asked Clover gently. The girl only shrugged but she did stop what she was doing briefly and stare out the window across the playground. 'It's just that when I looked at your notes from yesterday it seemed like you were upset about something and I couldn't work out why.'

'My mum told me about what happened. She heard about it from Olivia's mum,' said Sequoia. 'I couldn't help thinking about it.'

'Actually, it's been just the same for me,' said Clover gently. 'You know there's nothing to be worried about, don't you? Bad things happen in the world but we can't stop living our lives because something bad happens near to us. Even when something bad does happen there are hundreds of very good people ready to help and make everything better.'

'But what if it happened to Miss Robinson or Mr Flint or...*you*?' Sequoia's voice faltered and Clover realised with a creeping sense of embarrassment that Sequoia was principally afraid of something happening to her.

'You mustn't worry about anything like that,' said Clover fiercely. 'Your job is to enjoy your time here at school.' Her serious tone elicited a nod of agreement from Sequoia but she stared out into the playground again. 'If there's anything that bothers you, anything at all, please tell me about it, won't you?' asked Clover. Sequoia nodded with conviction and focused on her work once again. Troubled by the girl's worries, Clover stood up and looked out of the window into the playground. She wished that nothing terrible would ever intrude into any of the children's lives, but that wasn't the way of the world. Then, something in the playground caught her attention.

What Clover had seen looked unremarkable at first glance. It was just a flower bed in which the blooms had been crushed, not an unusual sight in a place where a child might have stepped into the flowerbeds to fetch a lost football. However, it was the location of the flowerbed that gave Clover pause for thought and since it was her turn to go outside on playground duty, she realised that she would have ample time to examine it more carefully.

Clover pulled on her coat to follow the children outside. She had meant to investigate what she'd seen from the classroom window directly but she didn't make it very far across the playground before the children started bringing her their playground disputes to deal with.

The first was a complaint from a small boy from Ellie's class who ran up to Clover with the urgency of someone reporting a serious injury. Breathless with tears, he explained that someone in his class had *copied his game*. Sadly, this was not the kind of problem that even a United Nations consensus about copyright law could resolve. It wasn't really a problem with the game, of course, but about friendships and loyalty, neither of which could be helped by Clover sitting in judgement on the matter. Long experience had taught her how to coax the situation into resolving itself but there were no guarantees that anything would help right away. 'You must be an amazing game inventor,' said Clover gently. Her words of praise halted the tears immediately. 'I bet if you invent another part to your game then the others will want to ask you how it works and you can work out how to play together.' The small boy nodded at this seriously and without another word he turned on his heels and ran whooping off in the direction from which he'd come. Clover wondered if the whooping was a core component of his existing game or a new innovation that would have half the playground whooping in the next fifteen minutes. She proceeded towards the flower beds.

The second incident involved two girls whom she'd taught the previous year. Hayley and Claire were an inseparable pair who, on this occasion, simply wanted to show Miss Lightfoot their new dance. Clover could have deflected them very simply by asking them if they weren't a bit too old to still be showing off their dances to their teacher but she could imagine all too easily the kind of effect that would have on the girls. Clover understood that their real aim was to enjoy retreating into their childhood games just to see if they were still allowed. Clover gave them a warm smile and watched them engage in a set of quick synchronised twirls and hand flourishes. She'd only meant to indulge them for a moment but found herself properly amused and gave them a round of applause.

The final distraction that blocked Miss Lightfoot from reaching the disturbed flowerbeds was the appearance of Ellie with two steaming hot cups of tea. She carried them expertly across the playground, using an in-depth knowledge of the channels along which children suddenly came sprinting out of the toilets or the cloakrooms. Clover collected her tea gratefully and steered Ellie towards the back of the school building.

'How's it going?' she asked Ellie. 'Did you hear anything about Janet's meeting with the parents this morning?'

Ellie shrugged, 'I heard it was fine. Sandy and Bettina were both there and Mrs Chapman seemed delighted when they all agreed to blame the school's failings on Mr Fish.'

'Not to mention the murder,' said Clover.

'Quite! Apparently they tried not to mention that too much at all and just kept saying it was a police matter now.'

'What do you make of that?' said Clover changing the subject and pointing at the flowerbed she'd been trying to examine since playtime had begun.

'Oh that's a shame,' said Ellie, immediately concerning herself with the damage to the flowers. 'I love tulips. Whoever did that really didn't think about where they were treading. We should say something in assembly about it.'

'What if it wasn't one of the children though?' said Clover, 'Look at where the damage has been done.' Ellie stared at the trail of bright petals and then looked blankly back at Clover, not understanding what she was getting at.

'It's right underneath the window of the headteacher's office. Do you realise what that could mean?' Ellie shook her head and Miss Lightfoot started to explain.

18

Once she had seen the crushed flowers at close quarters, Clover found herself able to imagine a very different version of events on the night of the murder. It took a few minutes to walk Ellie through the details but Clover had spent years explaining complex ideas to the most distractable audiences imaginable and she was exceptionally good at her job.

'But if what you say is true, how will we prove it?' asked a stunned-looking Ellie.

Break time had seemed to pass in an instant and the school bell was already being paraded into the playground ready to be rung by two small children.

'I do have an idea of how we might find some proof,' said Clover. Come and eat your sandwiches in my classroom at lunchtime and we can work out a plan together.'

Ellie nodded, looking preoccupied with all that she'd just heard. Clover felt the same way but she forced herself to concentrate. 'Sequoia,' she called out, as she approached the line of children waiting to go indoors, 'would you take a message to Mr Flint for me please?' Sequoia nodded happily. 'Ask him to come to our classroom at lunchtime. I'm going to need his help with something.' As Sequoia ran off to deliver the message, Clover reflected that she was definitely going to need all the help she could get.

The following lesson passed in a blur and Tom and Ellie were both at her door before she'd even released her class for lunch. Sitting around her desk with their sandwiches, Clover talked Tom through what she thought had really taken place on the night of the murder. Tom looked worried. 'If this is true then it's going to upset a lot of people,' he said, 'and if it happened the way that you think, then it's almost a perfect crime. How can we convince anyone to believe us?'

'Trust me,' said Clover, 'we can do this. It's just like teaching a lesson. Our goal is for Detective Meadows to find out who really murdered Dr Winter. All we need to do is to present him with the information in an appropriate way and to give him the evidence he needs to understand the truth for himself.' Clover picked up some chalk and started to draw the details of exactly what she had in mind on the blackboard. By the end of lunchtime they had thought through every detail of their plan and all that remained was to carry it out.

Clover needed some time to make preparations and so Tom offered to look after her class for the rest of the afternoon. Mrs Clydesdale was surprised to see Clover out of class at the beginning of the afternoon session but when Clover asked to use the phone Mrs Clydesdale didn't make any further enquiries about what she was doing. Mrs Clydesdale would be able to overhear everything that was discussed anyway since the school office was far from private.

Clover took a seat by Mrs Clydesdale's desk and dialled a number from memory. It was the number on the card that Detective Meadows had given her but she knew that if she brought the card into view then Mrs Clydesdale wouldn't be able to resist asking what she was up to. Clover respected Mrs Clydesdale but she was by no means certain she could persuade her to join in and help with their little scheme, so for now she would need to be kept in the dark.

The phone rang, seemingly endlessly, before it was answered. 'Detective Meadows' desk,' said a voice. Clover's mind went blank. If it had been Meadows himself, Clover felt sure that she could have subtly asked him to meet her in her classroom at the end of the school day. Talking to a stranger meant she'd have to leave an explicit message to be sure that Detective Meadows was in the right place at the right time. Mrs Clydesdale would certainly take note of that. She had to think of some other way of making it happen. 'Hello?' asked the voice on the end of the line impatiently. 'Detective Meadows' line, is there anyone there?' Clover's thoughts spun as she searched for some way of disguising the conversation. Then she remembered the Detective's first name, a name that he shared with one of the boys in her class.

'Hello, yes, that's exactly who I'm trying to reach,' Clover answered nimbly, 'I'm Miss Clover Lightfoot at the School and I'm afraid there's a problem with Paul.'

There was a brief silence at the other end of the phone. 'Paul Meadows? Do you mean Detective Meadows?' the voice asked.

'Yes, precisely,' said Clover gratefully, 'I'll need to speak to him after class today so I was just calling to see if that's alright.' To Mrs Clydesdale's ear, Clover hoped it plausibly sounded like a naughty boy being kept back after school. Clover quickly passed on the information about when and where she wanted to meet the detective and, as if she tired of sitting in that position, she lifted the sturdy old telephone down onto her lap, being careful not to tug the wire out of the wall.

'I'll be sure he gets the message,' said the voice at the other end of the line.

'Thank you,' said Clover, discreetly holding down the tiny buttons on the phone to cut off the call. She continued speaking for the benefit of Mrs Clydesdale as the phone became silent at her ear. 'Paul means well, but he has to let other children join in with his game,' Clover said seriously. 'Yes,' she replied to the silent hand piece, 'that's fine. Other than this small matter, he is doing very well in class. See you later then, thank you.' She hung up the receiver properly and briskly returned the phone to its proper place on Mrs Clydesdale's desk.

'Oh, and Mrs Clydesdale,' said Clover, 'please could I borrow your copy of the falsified report that was sent to the school on the night of the murder? There's something about it that I really must check.' Mrs Clydesdale looked suspicious and began to ask a question but Clover cut her off. 'Some of the parents heard parts of the report being read out loud on the evening of the murder so I'll like to know exactly what it says in order to put their minds at rest.'

'Very well, Miss Lightfoot,' said Mrs Clydesdale, fetching the folded-up fax of the false report from a folder on the other side of her desk. Clover thanked Mrs Clydesdale courteously and made a swift exit to find Ellie and set up the final part of her plan.

19

After several days of continuous crisis, the school had an abandoned feel to it when a rather disgruntled Detective Meadows arrived to meet Clover at the end of the day.

'Miss Lightfoot,' nodded Meadows as he entered the classroom.

'Thank you for coming, detective,' said Clover sweetly. 'I trust my message wasn't too cryptic.'

'It was certainly unusual,' said Meadows. 'My colleagues couldn't tell whether you were about to put in a complaint or ask me out for dinner.'

Clover giggled nervously, 'I assure you, I didn't have either of those things in mind when I called you.' She was slightly unsure whether she'd been accidentally insulting but also equally worried that an apology might make things worse. It suddenly occurred to Clover that the only possible flaw in her plan might be her own temperament. She was well-practised at explaining things to children but when it came to other adults it was all too easy to second-guess herself and feel very awkward.

'So, why have you asked me here?' asked Meadows bluntly.

'We have some new evidence for you,' said Clover, setting aside all her fears and focusing on the task in hand. 'Would you come over here with me please?' Meadows followed her across to the large floor-to-ceiling windows and looked outside. Clover gave a wave. A hand waved back from a distant window on the other side of the playground. 'Do you know which room that window belongs to?' she asked Meadows.

'I'm sure I don't, Miss Lightfoot,' said Meadows, warily.

'It's the window of the headteacher's office and it's quite a large one, isn't it?' As Clover spoke, Ellie deftly climbed up onto the low window ledge of the headteacher's office and stepped through the open window. She walked along the window ledge for a few few feet then stepped easily down into the flower bed. She was careful to stay away from the places where the flowers had been already been crushed. She picked her way carefully between the plantings to avoid damaging them any further and stepped onto the tarmac of the playground beyond.

'As you see, it's perfectly easy for someone to climb in and out, even when they are dressed as smartly as Miss Robinson,' said Clover.

Ellie stood in the middle of the playground watching Clover and Meadows at the window. As Clover waved, Ellie climbed quickly back inside, stepping directly onto the window ledge with ease.

'There's just one more detail you need to know,' added Clover. 'Would you take a seat on the blue cushion?'

'I'm sorry, what?' Meadows objected, looking down at the large blue cushion that had been placed in the enclosed section of the reading corner. Pudding's hutch was right next to the cushion and Clover realised that Meadows was taken aback by the sight of the little honey-coloured bunny.

'Ignore Pudding! Believe me, he's far more scared of you than you are of him,' she said encouragingly, although this didn't seem entirely true because Pudding was staring straight at Meadows with a mildly vindictive look in his eye. 'I wouldn't ask if it wasn't important,' said Clover firmly. 'Please, take a seat on the blue cushion and look across at the headteacher's window.'

Meadows reluctantly dropped onto his knees before crawling onto the blue cushion, Sequoia's favourite place to sit. Once he was settled, he looked around him. The drape over the den shut out the glare from the classroom lights but it also gave him a very clear view through the window.

'I see,' he said, 'whoever was sitting here could have seen someone climbing in or out of the window.' He gave Pudding one more wary glance. 'I'll bite!' he said to the small rabbit, threateningly.

'Now, Miss Lightfoot, tell me who you think was climbing in and out of the headteacher's window on the night of the murder?'

'I'll introduce you,' said Clover and she waved out the window to Ellie who then turned and waved at someone else who was just out of sight. Barely a moment passed before there was a knock at the door. 'Keep quiet and take a note of everything you hear,' said Clover before pulling the drapes over Detective Meadows to conceal him inside the den.

Clover got to her feet and called out, 'Come in!'

The door opened and Tom stuck his head through. 'Miss Lightfoot?' he called.

Clover heard a slight rustling in the book corner that she presumed was Meadows getting his notepad out to write down

Tom Flint's name. She gave the bulge in the drapes a tiny kick and whispered, 'It's not him!' before turning to Tom.

'Mr Flint, has my guest arrived?'

'Mrs Chapman's here now,' said Tom, turning a rather unsteady smile towards Amanda Chapman, who came in through the door behind Tom, watching him with very cold eyes. 'Sorry that we were delayed in finding Miss Lightfoot,' said Tom, 'I thought she might have been waiting in one of the other rooms but it turns out she was here all along.'

'Thank you, Tom,' Clover interjected. 'Your timing couldn't have been more perfect.'

Clover had asked Tom to summon Mrs Chapman back to the school by telling her there was an urgent problem that they needed to discuss. Once she had arrived Tom had needed to stall until Clover could persuade Detective Meadows into his hiding place.

'Be seeing you!' said Tom, hastily backing away and closing the classroom door behind him.

'Miss Lightfoot,' said Mrs Chapman suspiciously, 'Why have I been called back here again? I was rather hoping that I'd seen the back of this school, for now at least.' She spoke with unguarded hostility and Clover met her tone of voice with equal frankness.

'That seems to be in keeping with your approach to inspecting schools, Mrs Chapman: visit briefly; make snap decisions that support your political agenda; and leave, all the while being unaccountable to anyone for your judgements.'

Far from taking offence at these accusations, Amanda Chapman smiled broadly. 'I have no problem with that arrangement at all. But if I were in your shoes, Miss Lightfoot, I'd be very careful about irritating me.'

Clover found herself taking a step backwards. There was something deeply repulsive about Mrs Chapman's cold self-confidence and although Clover had previously found it hard to believe it of her, Clover had no trouble imagining that the woman was capable of murder. She'd never thought it possible for someone to be as entirely cynical as Mrs Chapman appeared to be.

'Dr Winter certainly didn't think that school inspections should be like that,' said Clover.

Mrs Chapman chuckled throatily, 'Arthur was terribly naïve,' she said, 'that's why he let someone untrustworthy inside his house and ended up getting himself killed.'

'That may have been exactly what happened but I don't believe that the killer was Mr Fish,' said Clover, her voice finding a new edge of steel. She forced herself not to glance in the direction of the book corner; help was very close if she needed it but if she called upon Meadows too soon then she'd have lost her best chance to goad Mrs Chapman into a confession.

'Just who...' said Mrs Chapman, taking a menacing step forward, 'do you think...' she took another step, '...the killer might be, Miss Lightfoot?'

Clover turned towards the blackboard and picked up a piece of chalk. The very act of taking up her role as a teacher once again gave her strength, however, turning her back on Mrs Chapman was one of the most difficult things she'd ever done.

'Let's start with a question,' said Clover briskly. 'Who had the opportunity to murder Dr Winter on the night of the school play?' She wrote the words *Mr Fish* on the board. 'Certainly poor Simon Fish had the opportunity to commit the crime or Detective Meadows would never have allowed him to be taken in for questioning. So let's see how he could have done it.'

Clover didn't look back towards Mrs Chapman but she could sense the motionless figure with the icy stare behind her as she charted Mr Fish's movements on the night of the murder. She narrated Mr Fish's progress as she drew her diagram of the events.

'Distraught at discovering that his school was to be the subject of two bad reports simultaneously, Simon took himself off for a meditative walk only to run into Dr Winter stumbling home drunk. These facts are indisputable.'

Clover drew a stick figure to represent Dr Winter and a tiny line drawing of a fish alongside him to represent Mr Fish. 'However, if we are to believe that Mr Fish did the deed, then he would have had to enter Dr Winter's house, murder Dr Winter and then type the false report using Dr Winter's private notes, before sending that report to the school. He would have had to do this at the murder scene, escaping just before you arrived and mere moments before the police discovered you at the scene.'

'That does sound like the actions of someone unstable enough to commit a murder,' said Mrs Chapman. Her tone of voice was light and amused.

'However,' said Clover, picking up a different coloured piece of chalk. 'Let's examine someone else who had the opportunity to murder Dr Winter.'

Clover drew a question mark on the board and surrounded it with a circle. 'This mystery person would need to be unaccounted for at the time of the murder and...' Clover paused to look back at Mrs Chapman directly, 'perhaps they achieved this by locking themselves away in the headteacher's office. That would look like an alibi but only because nobody realised that it was relatively easy to come and go through the window without being noticed. It only takes five minutes to get to Dr Winter's house from here after all.'

Clover drew the encircled question mark close to the symbols for Dr Winter and Mr Fish. 'So let's say the murderer followed the luckless Mr Fish as he helped Dr Winter home. Once Mr Fish had left, the murderer paid a short visit to Dr Winter, perhaps to continue an argument that they had already begun in public.'

Clover crossed out the stick man with her chalk. 'Dr Winter was murdered and the culprit suddenly found themselves at the murder scene with blood on their hands, desperate to place the blame on someone else.' Clover drew a sketch of a little piece of paper next to the crossed-out stick man. 'The murderer chanced upon Dr Winter's book of notes on his desk along with the unfinished report that Dr Winter had been typing out, ready to be faxed to the school, and the murderer was struck by an idea. The murderer needed an alibi and they were far too astute to wait around at the scene of a murder that they had just committed. They took Dr Winter's report and notes with them and left the scene, returning...' Clover drew a dotted line that led all the way back to where she'd first drawn the question mark, 'here, to the headteacher's office where they were supposedly locked inside. This room happens to have a typewriter and a fax machine, identical to the one in the school office next door.' Clover drew four lines to enclose the question mark in a protective box. 'Safe in their hideaway, the murderer organised their alibi, typing the report and faxing it to the office next door. Perhaps they even made an anonymous call to the police to ensure that the body of Dr Winter would be found at just the right time.'

Clover rubbed out a gap in the square and drew an arrow leading outwards. 'Then the murderer emerged into a very public gathering and made quite certain that they were noticed. As they addressed the assembled parents and staff, the faxed report finished printing out. It contained objectionable comments that allowed the murderer to feign renewed rage at Dr Winter. This would give the murderer the chance to rush back to the scene of the crime just in time to apparently *discover* the murdered body before the police arrived, thus ensuring they were initially a suspect but then ruled out of the investigation entirely.'

Clover paused and examined her handiwork with satisfaction. She turned away from the blackboard to see Mrs Chapman beaming at her, displaying her small, sharp teeth.

'It seems that you are suggesting that I am the murderer. That is the most entertaining nonsense I've ever heard,' she mused. 'It's so ludicrous that I don't think I even need to bother denying it. You must despise me, Miss Lightfoot, to make such an accusation. But then maybe I'd despise someone who was about to smear my career with the kind of report that this school is going to be given. I can't blame you for trying to get even but, honestly, you will have to do better than that.'

Mrs Chapman advanced on Clover and plucked the piece of chalk from her fingers. She drew a long swirling line along the path of the question mark symbol on Clover's diagram. 'Such a long and tangled path with no real evidence to support it at all.'

'But if I am correct, the evidence should be easy to uncover now that we know where to look for it,' said Clover, not retreating an inch from Mrs Chapman. 'We've already found footprints in the flowerbed outside the headteacher's office.'

'Footprints in the flowerbeds? Miss Lightfoot, I am sure the children could have made those during playtime. They mean nothing at all.'

'Perhaps not,' said Clover, her eyes sharpening, 'but perhaps you weren't aware that the typewriter in the headteacher's office has a quirk which causes it not to type the letter R unless the key is struck very firmly. Suppose I told you that I found several errors in the false report that corresponded precisely with this quirk, confirming that the false report was typed in the headteacher's office, where you were, and not at the scene of the murder as we previously thought.'

To Clover's surprise Mrs Chapman did not look in the least bit threatened by this revelation but simply burst out laughing, 'You call that evidence?' she grinned. 'Your fun and games don't matter to me in the least because I will firmly deny having had anything to do with the falsified report.' She leaned in closer to Clover, 'but even if I had typed that report myself, I am quite certain that a few common typing errors would not offer any real proof that your version of the night's events is what took place.' There was no movement from the book corner and Clover took this to mean that Meadows didn't believe that the typographical errors would be enough proof to arrest Mrs Chapman either.

Clover blanched and looked down at her feet as Mrs Chapman chuckled to herself. 'What if there was a witness?' said Clover quietly. 'What if someone saw you come and go from the office window at a time that precisely matched the time of the murder.'

'If you had such a witness, we wouldn't be having this conversation at all because I would already be under arrest,' snapped Mrs Chapman but her grin had evaporated.

'If I had a witness who happened to be a child, do you think I'd put them in the middle of a murder investigation unless I absolutely had to?'

Mrs Chapman's eyes narrowed with a predatory zeal. 'That was very wise of you. It would probably be best for them if you told them to keep very quiet about what they'd seen because I would certainly make sure that your poor little witness had a most unpleasant time.'

'I don't see why you're making threats like that if you're innocent. You wouldn't need to give anyone a hard time unless you actually committed the murder.' said Clover, her own voice starting to tremble.

Taking up a reasonable tone once more, Mrs Chapman responded, 'Then for the sake of convenience, let us presume that I did murder Dr Winter.' Clover gasped and drew back but Mrs Chapman continued. 'Let us imagine that I did it because the old fool was a dinosaur who was in my way.' Mrs Chapman didn't blink, 'Don't be a fool and put an innocent child in my way too or, believe me, they will regret it and so will you.' Her voice chilled Clover to the bone and she felt tears appearing in the corners of her eyes.

The mood in the room had turned so sour, so quickly, that Pudding became positively wild with fear. He leapt at the side of his hutch, achieving a leap of entirely unexpected height and scurried quickly to hide behind Clover's ankles. As she gathered him up in her arms, Clover found her courage returning.

'But why?' asked Clover, 'Why do any of this?'

'I've already told you the reason, Miss Lightfoot. Your listening skills really are very poor. Dr Winter was in my way.'

'You're out of your mind,' whispered Clover.

'I am the head of Ofsted and that is all that matters,' replied Mrs Chapman, her eyes as bright as diamonds.

It was then that Pudding, ever sensitive to the mood in the room, began to struggle and panic in Clover's arms. Clover fumbled as she tried to hold him but he sprang in terror, using all the power of his strong hind legs in a desperate bid to escape. He leapt, breaking out of Clover's grasp and flew backwards through the air butting Mrs Chapman on the nose. She staggered backwards but was caught by Detective Meadows as he rose from his hiding place in the book corner at the sound of her horrified shriek.

Clover would never have suspected that Detective Meadows carried handcuffs somewhere in the pockets of his rumpled old suit. Moments later the steel bracelets snapped into place on Mrs Chapman's wrists and Detective Meadows held her firmly by the shoulders. At the sound of the commotion Tom Flint burst in through the door, closely followed by Ellie.

Detective Meadows' tone of voice was matter-of-fact as he read Mrs Chapman her rights. 'Amanda Chapman,' said Meadows, 'I arrest you for the murder of Dr Arthur Winter on the 3rd of March 1996 at his residence. You are not obliged to say anything unless you wish to do so but what you say may be given in evidence.' Then he turned to Clover. 'Miss Lightfoot, after what I've heard here tonight, I will endeavour to avoid asking a witness from your class to give evidence. I believe my notes and the leads you've given us tonight will be enough to charge and potentially convict the real murderer of Dr Winter.'

Clover smiled, 'That's excellent news, Detective Meadows because there never was a witness who saw Mrs Chapman climbing in and out of the headteacher's office. I simply asked the question, *what if there was*?' Clover met Mrs Chapman's eyes. 'I do believe that someone needs to improve their own listening skills,' she said. Mrs Chapman glowered at her but Meadows led her away without another word.

'Ellie,' said Clover. 'Do you have any chocolate left? I feel like we deserve some.' Ellie dashed out to grab some from her room.

'What happens now?' asked Tom, still struggling to take in the fact that Amanda Chapman had been arrested.

'Lots of things,' said Clover, 'but right now, I'd like to ask you out to dinner, Mr Flint. My treat. After I've finished with the chocolate, obviously.'

Epilogue: A New Beginning

It was the first assembly of the new school year and Mr Fish stood to address the whole school. The children were seated on the hall floor, cross-legged in neat rows while their teachers perched on plastic chairs. Mr Fish was wearing an orange robe in the style of the Dalai Lama. 'So,' he said, 'hands up if you went somewhere new over the summer holidays.' He raised his own hand as he said it. 'Can anyone guess where I went?' Some hands were raised and he chose one of the youngest children to suggest an answer.

'Was it the North Pole?' the child asked earnestly.

'Not quite, but it was certainly very chilly,' said Mr Fish.

Watching from the side of the hall, Clover wondered how long it would take the children to guess where Mr Fish had been. Perhaps one of the older children would be able to work it out, otherwise, Clover thought, it might be a very long assembly.

'Did you go to Africa?' asked someone from Year 4. That was quite a sensible suggestion Clover thought. She could certainly imagine Mr Fish's robes being worn in the Serengeti.

'No, not quite,' said Mr Fish, 'I went to an ancient temple in the mountains of Nepal. I went there especially to have a think all about the wonderful things we can do together in the new school year.'

Tom Flint met Clover's eyes from the other side of the hall and she matched his mild smile. She had no doubt he was imagining the same cartoonish adventures as she was: Mr Fish walking along a length of rice paper without tearing it and receiving the blessing of a Zen master; Mr Fish, sitting in a tiny stone cave and opening his eyes to the sound of cymbals; Mr Fish engaging in ferocious martial-art swordplay. Clover giggled silently as she looked at the children's faces.

Mr Fish continued, 'After the *unfortunate happenings* last term, I needed a very special rest and that's exactly what I got.' In the end, the police had never charged Mr Fish with any crime and the confusion that had reigned so completely after the murder of Dr Winter had vanished as quickly as it had arisen. All talk of the school being put into *special measures* had vanished with the arrest of Mrs Chapman and the appointment of Antonia Reynolds as the head of Ofsted in Mrs Chapman's place. Detective Meadows was the hero of the piece as far as the press were concerned and Clover was entirely content for that to be the case.

Mr Fish fed round, wooden prayer beads through his fingers as he beamed at the children. 'Sometimes we need adventures to learn more about ourselves,' he said, and Clover found herself nodding in agreement with this. 'Anyhow, a big part of our next adventure as a whole school will be to welcome our new Deputy Headteacher, Mr Billingham.'

Mr Fish gestured towards the slender, rather twitchy-looking man in a black suit, who smiled with his lips very firmly pressed together.

'As you all know, Mrs Clegg has gone on to become the headteacher of her own school and we all wish her all the very best of luck with that.' Seized with a sudden inspiration, Mr Fish said, 'Mr Billingham, would you like to tell us all something about yourself?'

'Certainly, Mr Fish,' Mr Billingham said smoothly, 'Good morning children!' he said to the whole hall.

On cue, there was an attempt at a response from the children, 'Good morning Mr...' they tailed off as they replied, their voices merging into an uncertain murmur as they each tried to remember his unfamiliar name.

'I'm Mr Billingham, your new Deputy Headteacher. But before I was a teacher, I did a very different job. What do you think that could have been?' he asked, working hard to engage the children's interest. Clover examined Mr Billingham and wondered what on earth the answer could be.

'Were you a podiatrist?' asked Michael, one of the boys in Ellie's new class. Ellie looked over at Clover and smiled. They both knew Michael's mother was a podiatrist and he tended to assume that the majority of the adult population had, at one time or another, worked in a foot-related area of healthcare.

Mr Billingham stumbled only a little at the suggestion, 'No, I'm afraid I wasn't a podiatrist,' he laughed, 'I wish!' he added, picking out another child to answer.

'Were you a nuclear scientist?' asked Marta, one of the new girls in Clover's class. She was studying Mr Billingham intently as she asked her question, as if scrutinising him for visible signs of scientific understanding.

'Not quite,' said Mr Billingham, 'I was actually something called a *management consultant*, which is a very special job. It's a lot like being a teacher, but instead of teaching lovely children like you, I was teaching adults who run all kinds of businesses. I would teach them all kinds of special lessons about how to do things much better than before.' He beamed at the teachers around the hall, 'Your headteacher, Mr Fish, heard about all the things I was doing and he thought 'Wouldn't it be wonderful if I could come and teach the teachers at your school something new too?' He smiled. 'I agreed with Mr Fish one hundred percent and I was very excited to be asked along to share my special knowledge with all of your teachers.' Clover could see Ellie's eyes bulge slightly at the self-importance of this. She rose from her seat and slipped behind the piano, gently signalling that the time set aside for assembly was coming to an end.

Mr Billingham seemed slightly taken aback at the lack of reaction to the good news he was presenting and he quickly continued before Mr Fish could take over and finish off the assembly. 'I really want everyone to feel like we're all together in a new adventure this year,' he said holding his arms out wide, 'and that's why I've made a special deal with Swanage House, the company that's running our fantastic Year 6 adventure holiday. And, do you know what they've agreed to?' he asked, like a stage magician building up to the best part of his trick. 'They have agreed to allow all the teachers to go along to their adventure holiday park for a special weekend of extra training and learning together, just at the same time as the Year 6 children are finishing their trip.' Clover exchanged glances with Tom Flint who taught the Year 6 class. He could only offer her a confused shrug, he clearly knew nothing about this.

'The very best part,' Mr Billingham announced with pride, 'is that the teachers will have a special discount price for their visit. So it won't be anything like as expensive as it would normally be for them to have such a life-changing weekend full

124

of exciting training activities.' Ellie played a minor chord on the piano, a chord that somehow contrived to sound perfectly indignant. Mr Billingham looked at her in surprise but she only smiled at him sweetly. Clover couldn't help but laugh.

Mr Fish started a faltering round of applause for Mr Billingham's speech which the children dutifully joined in with. Clover caught Sequoia giving her a gleeful look. Though Sequoia had moved up to Tom Flint's Year 6 class this term, she seemed absolutely delighted at the thought of her beloved Miss Lightfoot joining them for the last few days of the adventure holiday. Clover returned her smile but she didn't feel so sure about what had just been announced.

'Thank you so much, Mr Billingham, I can see all the teachers are very excited about this wonderful news,' said Mr Fish. Try as she might, Clover couldn't detect even the slightest trace of irony in Mr Fish's voice as he said these words and she shook her head involuntarily at the thought of the strange weekend ahead.

Ellie began to play the first joyful bars of Chopin's *Minute Waltz* on the piano.

'Ah,' said Mr Fish over the music, 'I hear that it's time for our new lessons to begin.' He nodded to the teachers, seemingly blind to the sceptical looks that they were giving him in return. Clover rolled her eyes but she smiled when she looked across at Tom Flint. After catching a murderer and saving the headmaster from prison, Clover thought that a weekend in the countryside couldn't possibly prevent her from getting on with some proper teaching.

CLOVER LIGHTFOOT WILL RETURN

In

**MURDER ON THE
PROFESSIONAL DEVELOPMENT WEEKEND**

Miss Clover Lightfoot Murder Mystery No.2

Investigate now at
goodreads.com/cloverlightfoot

18810687R00078

Printed in Great Britain
by Amazon